The Journey

The Rebekah Series: Book Two

JENIFER JENNINGS

To those whose journey seems too much to endure,
God's got an amazing adventure in store for you.

To Sebastian, enjoy the journey God has planned for
you.

Chapter 1

*"Abraham took another wife, whose name was
Keturah."*
-Genesis 25:1

Hebron, 2028 B.C.
Isaac

Joyous shouts rang out all around Isaac. It seemed
every ally within traveling distance had come to
celebrate his father's wedding feast. The gathering of

people filled the pastureland of Hebron to the brim. Sheep had been moved out of the way to make room for the festivity. Isaac would have rather gone with the livestock than to see his father united with a woman that wasn't his mother.

Keturah was nice enough for a concubine-turned wife. Her name meant incense, and it was fitting. She was sweet and kind, but she was no Sarah. Keturah was a wafting scent that, although enjoyed for a moment, passed quickly and was easily forgotten. Sarah was like a raging fire that burned big and bright. Isaac missed the fire of his mother. When her flame had gone out, his life seemed darker than night. At least the darkest night had stars, what did he have?

Isaac's stomach turned watching his father.

Abraham's delight could not be contained. He drank and laughed as if Sarah had never spent a day by his side. The old fool acted more like a twenty-year-old receiving his first bride, when in fact, the man was nearing his one hundred and thirty-seventh year. The majority of those years were spent with Sarah, who now lay barely cold in a hollowed-out cave in Machpelah.

Isaac emptied his wine cup and motioned for a servant to refill it.

The servant poured fresh wine into the clay cup as Isaac watched on. He didn't care that he had lost count of how many he'd emptied since the feast began. In one fluid motion, he downed the drink and handed the cup to the servant. He wiped his wet lips on the back of his sleeve and headed toward his father.

"Ahh, my son." Abraham flung his arms open wide. "Come to congratulate the bridegroom?"

With liquid courage lighting a fire in his veins, Isaac set his feet wide. "I've come to give the bridegroom a piece of my mind."

Abraham's dark eyes turned to iron. "Please, son," He put his hand on his son's shoulder. "Let's just enjoy this day."

"Enjoy?" he spat the word. "My *ima's* body lies motionless in a cave freshly hewn, and you celebrate her by taking this concubine for a wife as if *Ima* never existed."

Abraham put his free hand on Isaac's other shoulder and squeezed. "Please, son. Don't do this."

Even under the pressure of his father's hold, Isaac felt the world shift sideways. "I will speak my mind."

"You will hold your tongue."

Isaac lifted his arms between his father's and broke free of his hold. "You need someone in your life that will speak truth. Your servants do nothing but agree with you."

The scurry of nearby servants stopped to look to their master.

Abraham waved them on.

"How can you betray *Ima* like this?" Isaac felt his strength wane and tears fill his eyes.

"I'm not betraying your mother."

"We buried her only days ago, and now we stand here feasting your new wife." He dipped his head to Keturah in an exaggerated bow, but the motion caused him to stumble.

A pair of strong arms caught him before he landed in the grass.

Isaac looked up into the face of Eliezer, his father's oldest and most trusted servant.

"Master Isaac, may I have a word with you?"

"I'm not done speaking with my *abba*." Isaac attempted to pull his arm free, but the servant's grip proved too much.

"It will just take a moment." Eliezer yanked Isaac away allowing him to stumble along.

"If you don't unhand me, servant, I will see to it that—"

"You will do no such thing." Eliezer finally freed him when they were far enough away not to be overheard. "For in the morning, your head will ache too much to remember anything you said this day."

Isaac rubbed his sore arm. "You know nothing of what I shall remember."

"I've seen too many fools lose their tongues and more over too much wine."

"*Abba* is the fool."

He crossed his arms over his chest. "Why? Because he chooses to make an honest woman out of Keturah?"

"Because he is replacing my *ima*, his wife."

"Your mother is no longer here."

"What does that matter?"

Eliezer sighed. "It matters to a man who is grieving and lonely."

"I'm lonely!" Isaac barked. "I'm grieving. What remedy is there for my pain?"

The servant kept still.

"You see, not even you, the wise Eliezer, can answer."

"I cannot answer because each man must grieve in his own way. Your father has chosen his. Keturah has been a loyal concubine since your mother fell ill years ago. She has done nothing to usurp her role. None of the fault can be laid at her feet."

A tremor went through Isaac's body. Though the wine fueled his anger and bitterness, the words of Eliezer cooled their flames. He pushed his hand through his disheveled hair. "You're right." He sighed and held his head. "I need to apologize to her."

"And to your father."

Isaac hardened for a moment before conceding. "And *Abba*."

"Good boy."

With staggering steps, Isaac returned to his father's side. "Forgive me, *Abba*. My words were unnecessarily harsh. I shouldn't have spoken to you in such a manner during your wedding feast."

Abraham reached over and patted his arm. "You are forgiven, my son. Now, go enjoy yourself."

He gave a short nod to Keturah. "May Elohim

bless your union."

She closed her eyes and dipped her head.

As Isaac made his way through the crowd, he waved off the offerings of food and more drink. The overwhelming sense of joy and merriment of the crowd grew too strong for him. Without word to anyone, he retreated to the place where the flocks had been taken.

Among the bleating of sheep and various other livestock, Isaac found a stillness that was all his own. He'd rather spend every moment of the day among those who followed him than plaster on a false smile with those who only sought his father's wealth.

He checked on each creature as he wound his way through the stalls. The animals yielded to his touch and none of them sought to betray him. They cared nothing for riches as long as their bellies were full.

His female dog trotted over to his side and rubbed against him.

"I don't understand why *Abba* would want to get married at such an advanced age anyway, Tira." He scratched her head. "I'm thirty-seven and he's never even discussed my betrothal." His gaze stretched over the open field before them. "We've been so many places and seen our fair share of what this vast land has to offer."

Tira huffed at him.

"Don't get me wrong, the women here are quite beautiful. It's just that they seem so...well...empty. They have no fire, no life in them." He stroked his dog's thick fur. "I'd like a wife more like *Ima*. She had such life." Dampness blurred his vision and his head started to pound. He rubbed his forehead. "I guess this life of travel wouldn't be very fair to a woman from Canaan. They have wonderful stone homes to protect them. Not like us who sleep in tents and travel wherever Elohim tells *Abba* to go."

Tira licked his hand.

"Yet, *Abba* has selected a woman from among them for himself." He sighed and leaned his forearms on the makeshift gate to watch the evening sun start its descent. "I'm the chosen seed of this new promised line, yet without a wife and with *Ima* now gone, it stops at me. Maybe Hagar was right, maybe Elohim will choose her son, Ishmael, over me. He's already married and has born sons."

The large dog put her paws on the gate and pressed her cold, wet nose to his cheek.

He nuzzled her back, then allowed his gaze to return to the distance. "I don't see much life here now for me. *Abba* will be too busy with his new wife and I'm old enough to be on my own. Perhaps it's time to be moving on." Isaac rubbed his dog's head hard enough to cause her ears to flop back and forth. "Maybe we'll pay a visit to my brother, Ishmael."

"Ishmael?" a deep voice caused Isaac to turn around. Abraham stood about a stone's throw away. "When I couldn't find you at the feast, I assumed you'd be here. What were you saying about Ishmael?"

Isaac leaned back against the wall. "I'm planning a visit to see him."

"May I ask why?"

He looked at his sandals. "I think it's time I took my leave of this place. You will need space for your new life, and I need to start mine."

Abraham took a step closer. "You're leaving?"

He nodded. "It's time."

"But where will you go?"

"To see Ishmael first. There are plenty of lands down near Beerlahairoi. Perhaps I'll settle there for a while."

"Have you sought Elohim in this matter?"

Isaac paused. The truth was Elohim had never spoken to him as He spoke with Abraham. The invisible, practically unknown deity had chosen to remain silent to everyone except his father. Even if Isaac had taken the time to seek guidance, he wasn't sure if he'd receive an answer. "No."

"I think you should. Such decisions should not be made on a mind soaked in wine."

The throbbing in his head reminded Isaac of the many cups he had emptied at the feast. He rubbed his forehead with the heel of his palm. "Maybe you're right."

Abraham gave a sharp nod and left without another word.

Isaac turned around and set his arms back on the gate to watch as the first star came out. "Elohim, I don't know if You're listening, but *Abba* says You do. You probably won't speak to me like You do to him, but I am asking for Your guidance." He rubbed at the increasing ache in his head. "I don't really know how You will respond, but I believe I should leave Hebron and head south. There is more room for me there and perhaps a new life."

The stillness was invaded only by the lingering sounds of the wedding feast still taking place in the open field.

He sighed. No voice broke through the night to reach him.

Chapter 2

"In the beginning, God created the heavens and the earth."
-Genesis 1:1

Emar, 2025 B.C.
Rebekah

The only home Rebekah had ever known was a day's journey behind, and her future home seemed like a lifetime across the desert.

Excitement over her family's security was now met head-on with the cold fact that her life now yielded to the will of a stranger. At least Kishar and Laban were safe and sound back in Haran. Her mother and brother had enough precious jewels and gold to provide a comfortable life. Perhaps even a thriving one if Laban made smart choices with the wealth they had been handed. The image of his honey-crusted beard and guiltless glance wrapped around her heart. Would his hunger lust prove to be her family's undoing?

Rebekah shook away the dreadful thought. There was nothing she could do to order her brother's steps. Only he could walk the path before him as she walked the one before her.

She glanced behind her to find her nurse Deborah and her handmaid Hadiya. What had she hauled them into? Under the hand of Abraham and Isaac, what life could she hope to provide them?

Her gaze drifted to the firelight. She watched as the flames danced free and unencumbered, like the Euphrates River they had crossed only hours ago. Both could be unstoppable forces causing even the land to yield to them. If properly handled and contained, they could be used for survival. Which future lay ahead of her?

She closed her eyes and fought against the tears that stung them. Her heart ached for her father's embrace. If he hadn't gotten injured, he'd be leading the family, and Rebekah would have been able to live out her days among her flocks. But his death had left a need. A need she alone couldn't fill. Once the opportunity came to fill it, she jumped on the camel and left everything she'd known. Now the void she was left with and the path she'd been forced on lay ahead of her with more questions than answers.

"So, how much do you know of your Great Uncle Abraham?" Eliezer's voice snatched her from the darkness of her despair.

She looked up to see his shining eyes staring down

at her. The firelight seemed only to heighten their youthful appearance. Though, with as much gray as was painted in his long beard, she suspected he was older than most of her uncles.

He handed her a bowl of stew.

"Very little actually." She accepted the meal with a nod and set it next to her feet. Hunger was the last thing on her mind. "He was a forbidden topic among my family."

"Oh." The servant settled down on the other side of the fire. "And why is that?"

Rebekah filtered through the pieces of conversations she'd heard about the estranged family member. "My *dods* believe he abandoned them to chase after an invisible and unknown god."

Eliezer took a bite from his bowl and chewed it longer than necessary. "And this 'invisible and unknown god', do you know of Him?"

She shook her head. "He was also a forbidden topic."

"I see." He enjoyed the rest of his meal seemingly unbothered by the silence that hung over the group.

Rebekah glanced at the four younger men who accompanied Eliezer. They ate in haste and kept their eyes searching around them. Each of them was drastically different, yet they all seemed as broad as they were tall. They were like chiseled boulders cut with experienced hands. She imagined them as four stone walls surrounding the caravan like a fortress. She suspected that had been the sender's intent.

"Where are my manners?" Eliezer rubbed his face. "I should have introduced you to your guard." He pointed to the man closest to him. "This is Layth, Taj, Dov, and Meir." As he gestured down the line, each man bowed toward her.

She bowed back. "Thank you for your service."

Their eyes returned to the distance.

"They are the best of Abraham's guard. I can assure you, my dear, you are in very safe hands."

"I have no doubts." She glanced behind herself. "This is my nurse, Deborah." She reached behind and squeezed her hand. "And Hadiya, my handmaid."

Eliezer nodded to the women.

"They are happy to help in any way possible."

"I'm sure they are." He smiled. "Now, I'd like to tell you about my master." He set down his empty bowl and folded his hands in his lap. "But in doing so, I'd also have to tell you about the God he serves. Now, you were probably taught that the gods created humans by mixing clay with the blood of a rebellious deity named We-ilu. He had been specially slaughtered for the occasion, yes?"

Rebekah swallowed hard and nodded. It was not one of her favorite stories, but his summary was accurate.

She thought back to her last trip to the temple of her Goddess Inanna. The empty-handed statue who'd left her in the hands of a flash flood and a thief, had ripped off her father's leg, and then ripped the entire man from her life. A shiver crawled its way up her back.

"I think it would help if I shared with you some of our stories. Stories that stretch much further back and have deeper truths than what you've been told." The old servant searched her with his eyes in the quiet. "If you'd like, I can start at the beginning. We do have a long journey ahead of us. Plenty of time to talk."

She waved for him to continue.

"In the beginning," Eliezer looked into the clear sky, "Elohim created the heavens and the earth. His spirit moved over the face of the waters. He called light into the darkness and separated the two into night and day. He divided the waters from dry land and yielded all kinds of plants. He filled the whole earth and sea with many different kinds of animals. One such place was a garden called Eden."

As his words flowed like a calm stream, Rebekah's mind conjured images of plants and animals living together in a beautiful garden. His voice reminded her of her uncle. "My *Dod* Uz used to tell me stories of Inanna and a Huluppu tree that she planted in her garden."

"Ahh, in the garden that I speak of there was planted a tree also, but we shall arrive there in time." His eyes sparkled. "All the things Elohim had made were good, but He wasn't done creating. He scooped some of the dust from the ground and formed a man." Eliezer dug his fingers into the sand and poured some into his other hand. "Then Elohim breathed on the man imparting life and a soul into him." He blew the pile of sand into the fire causing the flames to dance wildly and set some pieces of sand ablaze.

"Elohim put the man in the garden and allowed him to tend it. He brought forth all the animals and let the man name each one."

Rebekah reached over and scratched her dog, Zami behind the ear.

The dog rubbed into her palm for more attention.

"But the man found none like him. So, Elohim caused a deep sleep to come over the man." Eliezer waved his hand over his eyes and pretended to sleep.

A smirk tugged at Rebekah's lips, but she fought the urge. She imagined herself sitting in her mother's warm kitchen listening to Deborah's lessons and around the table listening to her uncles share stories. The hope of simpler times was far behind her.

"While the man slept, Elohim removed a rib from the man."

At the mention of ribs, she rubbed her old injury. The bouncing camel had revived the ache from the break she sustained trying to save a sheep in the flash flood. She imagined having a rib taken away would be just as painful.

"With the rib, Elohim formed a woman. That's why you women are much stronger." He winked. "We men were created from dirt, but you women were crafted from bone."

She smiled despite herself.

"Elohim placed the woman next to the man in the garden. The woman slowly opened her eyes against the bright light and blinked several times before searching around her. She had no memory; she had no knowledge of what happened before that moment. She glanced at her flesh and then reached to touch a blade of grass. Everything was new. Everything was fresh and bright.

"She slowly raised her head and brought herself up to sit. So many sounds and sights overwhelmed her. She didn't know what to look at first. She inhaled the sweet smell of life and then held onto it, never wanting to let the moment pass.

"A groan behind her caught her attention and she twisted to see what had made the noise. She saw something lying in the grass beside her. It was long and strange, but appeared similar to herself. She edged closer and slowly reached to touch it.

"The creature rolled over, and she saw him. She caressed the contours of his strong face. She traced his lips and nose. She felt his warm breath on her fingertips. As she leaned over the handsome creature, his eyes opened and he smiled up at her.

" 'Hello there,' he said. 'I am called Adam. And I shall call you… Eve. For you were taken from me.' Adam reached over to his side.

"Eve saw a faint line across his side. She reached out and traced the line with her fingers.

" 'Elohim has taken you from my bone and made you flesh of my flesh.'

"Eve looked deep into Adam's eyes. 'Elohim?' she asked.

" 'Come sit with me.' Adam smiled deeply as he sat up.

"Eve obeyed and looked around and then back at Adam.

" 'Just wait,' he assured her.

"After a few moments, a form moved toward them.

"Eve glanced at Adam.

" 'It's Him.'

"Eve rose slowly and waited for the form to come closer.

"Light encircled the being who stood before Eve. He was so beautiful. She thought Adam had been beautiful, but Elohim was magnified with so much radiance, it took her breath away. His white, curly hair and bronzed feet shone bright. And His eyes. His eyes were like fire which pierced through her and in the same moment shone with absolute love.

" 'Eve, my daughter,' Elohim said as He drew her to Himself.

" 'Adam,' Elohim called the man closer. "She is yours. She shall be your helper and you shall be her provider and guide. Love her, Adam. I've made her especially for you.

"Elohim took Adam's hand and placed it together with Eve's. 'I'm giving you to each other. I'm leaving her in your care, Adam. Take care of her as you do for your own body and love her.' " Eliezer paused and watched Rebekah. "The very first man and woman Elohim ever created. The two would become the father and mother of us all."

Rebekah leaned forward. "And the tree?"

Eliezer nudged Layth with his elbow. "We've got a bright one here. Doesn't miss a thing."

The guard nodded a simple agreement.

"The tree. Of course. Well, Adam took his wife through the entire garden, showing her all Elohim had created for them. When they reached the very center of the garden, Eve noticed a large tree. Adam explained that it was the tree of the knowledge of good and evil and was off limits to them. Elohim had told them not to eat of the tree or they would die."

"Die?" Rebekah found herself caught up in the story. "Why would Elohim plant a tree that would cause their deaths?"

"That is the same question Eve asked Adam. It was Elohim's rule. They had the entire garden and all the fruit in it to eat. Elohim had only given them one rule to follow; the fruit of that one tree must not be eaten."

"But why?"

"Sometimes Elohim does things that are part of His plan without giving us the reasons."

"Did Adam and Eve enjoy their garden?"

"For a time." Eliezer looked to his sandals. "Until the day that Eve ate from the forbidden tree."

"She did?"

He nodded. "One day, Eve was walking in the garden. As the day grew late, Eve's stomach growled. She looked up to see the forbidden tree. The fruit looked so delicious. As Eve turned to find her husband, she heard a strange sound.

" 'Eve,' a soothing voice called.

"She turned to see a large serpent walking toward her.

" 'I heard your stomach. Are you not hungry?'

" 'Why yes, I am. In fact, I was going to pick something for myself.'

" 'Why not eat the fruit here?' The serpent patted the trunk of the large tree.

"Eve shook her head. 'Elohim said we can't eat of that fruit.'

"The serpent chuckled. 'Didn't Elohim say you could eat fruit from any tree in the entire garden?'

"Eve thought for a moment. 'He said we could eat of any tree in the garden, but we can't eat from the tree in the middle of the garden.' She pointed to the tree. 'Elohim said we shouldn't eat or even touch it otherwise, we'll die.'

"The serpent stroked the bark of the tree. 'You will not die. Elohim only told you that because He knows if you eat this fruit, your eyes will be opened and you will be a god because you will know good and evil.'

"Eve's stomach protested. She looked at the ripe fruit which hung low on the branches. Taking a step closer, she reached up and plucked a piece. She held the fruit to her nose and inhaled its sweet savor.

" 'See, you shall not die,' the serpent hissed.

"Eve closed her eyes and opened her lips. As she bit into the crisp fruit, a burst of sweet juices flooded her mouth. She chewed the bite and then opened her eyes. The beautiful garden she had grown to love seemed to dim. She glanced over at the serpent and watched the creature's mouth twist into a vicious grin.

"For the first time ever, Eve was terrified. She looked down at her flesh and noticed she was exposed and felt the need to cover herself. As she frantically grabbed at mud and leaves, the serpent walked away chuckling to himself.

"She sat down on the grass and thought about what she had done. Then Eve heard something rustle. At first, she thought it was the serpent coming back, but then she heard Adam's voice, 'Eve?'

" 'Here I am.' She rose slowly from the bushes.

" 'Eve? What's wrong? Why are you covered in mud?'

"Eve thought quickly. 'Come here, my husband. I have something to share with you.' She handed him the fruit of which she had taken a bite. 'It is the most delicious thing I have ever eaten.'

"Adam took the fruit. He brought it to his lips and took a bite. 'It is good. I don't think I've eaten this before. Where did you get it?'

"Eve pointed to the tree.

"Adam looked down at the fruit and then back at her. 'What have you done? Elohim told us not to eat from that tree.'

"Eve watched the beautiful color drain from her husband's face. Adam spit out the fruit, but it was too late. He looked down at his flesh and at his wife who was covered with mud and leaves.

" 'Adam, now we can be like Elohim.'

" 'We're naked, Eve!'

" 'Take some of these and cover yourself.' She rubbed his body with mud and leaves.

"As Adam tried desperately to cover his shame, they both heard rustling.

"Adam looked up at the sky and saw how late it was getting and the air had grown cool. 'He's coming.' Adam pulled his wife's arm. 'Come on, we need to hide.'

"They ducked behind a nearby bush.

" 'Adam?' Elohim called.

"Eve's breath quickened as she held onto Adam's arm and buried her face into his shoulder. Adam placed his finger over his lips. Eve's eyes began to water, and she closed them in an attempt to erase what was happening.

"Elohim's steps drew closer to them and then the brush moved. 'Adam? Why are you hiding?'

"Adam stood. 'I heard your voice in the garden and was afraid and I'm naked so I hid myself.'

"Elohim's eyes burned bright. 'Who told you that

you were naked? Have you eaten from the one tree I told you not to eat?'

"Adam pointed down at Eve. 'The woman You gave me; she gave me the fruit to eat.'

"Eve stood and took a step away from them.

" 'What have you done?' Elohim asked her.

"Eve shook her head as she backed up further. 'It was the serpent. He tricked me, and so I ate.'

" 'Serpent,' Elohim called.

The serpent stepped from the bushes.

" 'Because you have done this thing, you are cursed above every creature. Upon your belly you shall go.' Elohim pointed at the creature. The serpent's arms and legs fell off and withered on the ground.

"Eve heard the serpent screech as he threw himself on the grass.

" 'And dust shall you eat all the days of your life. And I will put hostility between you and the woman. Between your seed and her seed. Her seed shall bruise your head, and you shall bruise his heel."

"Eve's skin crawled as she watched the serpent slither away.

" 'Eve,' Elohim's sharp voice caught her attention. She gulped as she tried to fight looking into His scorching eyes.

" 'I will greatly multiply your sorrow and your conception. In deep sorrow will you bring forth children. And your desire will be toward your husband and he shall rule over you.'

"Eve began to weep."

Rebekah wanted to weep too. She thought of Inanna and how the Goddess longed for a throne. Rebekah's tears had flown freely in sympathy for a Goddess who wanted her rightful place. Her heart nearly broke for the woman named Eve who had been deceived into eating the forbidden fruit. Allowing the dampness to run down her cheeks, she looked at Eliezer. "Did they die?"

He nodded. "But Elohim wasn't finished with them yet. He turned to Adam. 'Because you have hearkened unto the voice of your wife and have eaten of the tree, of which I commanded you not to eat, I will curse the ground for your sake. In sorrow, you shall partake of it all the days of your life. Thorns and thistles shall take over the earth and you shall eat the herb of the field.

" 'In the sweat of your face shall you eat bread until you return to the ground. For out of it were you taken and unto dust shall you return. Now, you must take your wife and leave the garden.'

" 'But…' Adam reached for Him.

"Elohim held up His hand. 'This is how it must be.'

"Eve noticed two young lambs prance into the open field behind Elohim.

"Moving into the meadow, Elohim beckoned the animals to Himself. He picked them up and took them back to Adam and Eve.

"They watched as Elohim searched the ground for

a stone. Then, to their horror, He struck the creatures and placed each at their feet.

"Eve watched as He took a sharp rock and removed the skin from the animals. Fashioning the skins into two garments, Elohim removed the leaves from Adam and Eve and placed the skin clothes on each of them as more suitable coverings.

"Eve's stomach turned over at the sight of the blood which covered Elohim's hands and His white robe.

" 'Now, it's time to leave the garden.'

"As they left, Elohim set a gate outside the garden with two large angels armed with flaming swords to guard the entrance. He stood before them and told them, 'The entire world is yours. Work the ground and multiply. Fill the earth with your kind and subdue the world.' "

Rebekah thought in silence. "So, they didn't die?"

"Eventually they did. They missed out on the garden and the life Elohim had for them. Instead, they spent their days laboring in the harsh land that often was unyielding to them."

Inanna and her Huluppu tree now dimmed to Rebekah in the light of Eve and her fruit tree. The old story that had been a balm to her soul on more than one occasion now seemed foreign.

Like Eve, Rebekah too felt banished from her home and part of her wished to turn the caravan around and return to her family. But doing so would mean giving back their security. She sighed. She too must face the unknown path ahead of her as Eve had done.

Chapter 3

"Now Adam knew Eve his wife, and she conceived
and bore Cain, saying, 'I have gotten a man with the
help of the LORD.' "
-Genesis 4:1

Emar, 2025 B.C.
Rebekah

Rebekah splashed a handful of fresh water onto her face to wash off the sand. With one more city behind them, and who knew how many more ahead, she took every opportunity to revel in being clean from the dust of travel.

Since leaving home, the strange dream had returned. The meadow. The divided path. The well. The voice. All still haunted her even though she had followed the stranger. Long hours atop a camel left her too much time to think. She feared she'd go mad before reaching her betrothed. Her path had been chosen for her, why did the voice still call?

Eliezer's men stood nearby keeping an eye on the horizon while the old servant took a long drink from his freshly-filled pouch.

Rebekah rubbed water on her arms. "Are you going to tell me more about Eve?"

"She intrigues you?" He took another gulp.

"Very much."

"Well," he sat on the edge of the short stone wall, "Adam and Eve had two boys. The first they called Cain and the second was named Abel. They grew into men and learned alongside their parents how to tend the ground and care for flocks."

Rebekah's heart ached at the mention of flocks. She wondered how hers was fairing under the leadership of her brother. It was nearing time to prepare the tablelands. Would he listen to the advice of their uncles better than he had listened to hers?

"One day, Adam called his sons to sacrifice before Elohim. Abel enjoyed caring for sheep and chose his best one to present."

Rebekah smiled. She liked Abel.

"Cain, on the other hand, preferred to work the ground. He was so proud of his harvest that he chose from the last of his fruits as his sacrifice, choosing to keep the best for himself."

Cain reminded her of Laban. She remembered the greedy look in his eyes as her dowry and gifts were laid before him.

Eliezer dipped a rag into the water, twisted it, and

wiped the sweat from his forehead. "At the stone altar Adam had built, each presented their gifts. Cain arranged his grains and fruits carefully on the flat stones. Abel removed his sharp blade from his belt, slit the throat of his best sheep, and laid the body on the altar.

"The sky lit up with fire which came down and consumed only Abel's offering. Cain looked over at the smile on his brother's face. Content that his offering had been accepted, Abel returned to the field. Cain glanced at his carefully arranged gift and then up to the sky. He waited as the sun moved across the firmament. But no fire came down.

"Cain stood over his offering. His face grew hot and his breath quickened. He reached up and wiped the food off the altar and onto the dust with a grunt. He stomped away. He was sitting in the grass when Abel found him later in the day.

" 'Cain, what are you doing out here?' his brother asked.

" 'Thinking. Leave me alone.'

" 'I'm sorry Elohim didn't accept your offering.'

" 'I said to leave me alone.'

" 'There is always the next offering. Maybe I could help you—"

" 'Why can't you just leave me alone?' Cain flew at his brother.

"They rolled on the ground.

" Abel yelled at him to cease, but Cain didn't listen

to his brother's pleas. Cain sat on top of his brother and grabbed his covering. He lifted him up and shoved him back to the ground.

"Abel continued to plead for relief, but Cain reached around. His fingers found a large stone and he held it high in the air.

" 'Please don't!' Abel screamed.

" 'Just be quiet!' Cain smashed the rock into his brother's face.

"Cain huffed as he rolled off his brother. He sat for a moment staring down at his bloody hand. Then he glanced over at his brother's still body. 'Abel?' He shook his brother, but Abel didn't wake. Cain stood. 'What have I done?' He knelt and rubbed his hands in the dirt. 'All I wanted was for him to be quiet. If he would have just left me alone, I wouldn't have…' He rose and left his brother's body where he lay."

Rebekah looked into the deep well. Her heart ached for the young man. She disliked her brother a lot of times, but hate never filled her to the point of harm. How Cain must have been broken.

"As night came upon the home of Adam and Eve, the mother knew something was not right. It was custom for the boys to return before dark. She glanced up at the dark sky for the hundredth time.

" 'I'm sure they lost track of time,' Adam offered.

" 'I'm sure you're right, it's just…' Eve paused. 'Oh good, here they come.'

" 'See, I told you not to worry.'

"Eve watched Cain's shape come closer to the tent. 'Cain,' she said, searching behind her firstborn. 'Where is Abel?'

"He walked past her, ignoring the question.

" 'Cain,' Eve said sternly. 'I asked you, where is your brother?'

"Cain whipped around. " 'Am I my brother's keeper?'

"Eve looked over the tense body of her son. 'Cain,' she looked down at his crusted hands. 'What has happened?'

"Adam stepped closer. 'What is it, son? Where is Abel?'

"Eve heard steps outside the tent and she ran. 'Abel, thank... Elohim?'

"Adam stepped outside the tent to see Elohim standing before Eve.

"Elohim walked past both of them and stood in front of Cain. 'Where is your brother Abel?'

" 'How am I supposed to know? Am I his keeper?' Cain spat the words.

" 'Cain,' " Eve scolded.

"Elohim shook His head. 'What have you done? Your brother's blood cries out to me from the ground.'

" 'What?' Eve screeched. 'Where is Abel?'

"Adam grabbed his wife.

" 'Abel,' Eve cried. 'I want my son.'

"Adam held her tight.

"Elohim looked back to Cain.

"Cain folded. 'I'll take you to him.'

"He guided the three of them to Abel's body in the middle of the field.

"Eve ran over and cast herself on top of her son. 'No!' She scooped the still body into her lap and began to stroke his head. 'Wake up, Abel. Please wake up.' She rubbed her face in the boy's hair.

"Elohim turned to Cain who stood watching his parents. 'Now you are cursed on the earth which has opened her mouth to receive your brother's blood from your hands. When you till the ground, it will not yield to you. A fugitive and a vagabond you will be in all the earth.'

" 'No!' Eve yelled. 'You can't take him too.'

"Cain's eyes filled with tears. 'My punishment is greater than I can bear. You have driven me out from the face of the earth and from Your face shall I hide. If You make me a fugitive and a vagabond, then everyone who finds me will try to kill me.'

" 'Please,' Eve begged. 'Don't take away my son.'

"Elohim looked at her and nodded. 'Whosoever shall slay Cain, vengeance shall be taken on him sevenfold.' Elohim reached down into the dirt which was stained with Abel's blood. He took His finger and drew on Cain's forehead. 'This mark shall be a symbol unto all who come across you. So all will know you are cursed in the land.'

" 'No! Eve reached for her son. 'Please don't send him away.'

"Adam comforted his wife. 'It has to be done, Eve. Just as we had to leave the garden because of our sin, so Cain has to leave because of his.'" Eliezer wiped his face again with the damp rag in his hand.

Rebekah didn't move or blink as she soaked in the servant's words. "Tell me that's just a story. A tale to keep boys from wrestling each other to harm."

"I'm afraid it's true."

"What happened to him?"

"Cain? Well, he left as Elohim commanded. When the land didn't yield to him, he built a great city. He became a new people, separated from his family."

"And Eve?"

"She and Adam went on to have lots more children and to see their children's children. They mourned Abel and Cain, but obeyed Elohim's command to fill the earth." He squinted at the rising sun. "I'll tell you more later. We need to get this caravan moving."

Rebekah moved to follow him to the waiting camels. She imagined poor Eve and how her heart must have shattered at seeing two of her sons be stripped away in a single day. Faces of family members Rebekah didn't see before she left flashed in her mind. She would miss them terribly. It seemed she had been stripped away as well to wander the desert to places unknown to her.

Chapter 4

"Seeing that Abraham shall surely become a great and mighty nation, and all the nations of the earth shall be blessed in him?"
-Genesis 18:18

Hebron, 2027 B.C.
Isaac

Isaac walked among his growing flocks. A year after his father's wedding feast, life had shifted into a new routine. He stayed in the fields as much as possible among the hired hands and far away from his father's new wife.

Without a command, Tira rounded the sheep in tighter toward Isaac. At least one woman in his life knew how to stay on his good side. The golden beauty bounded to him for a rewarding pat on the head for her efforts.

"Good girl. Keep them close."

The female dog licked his hand and trotted off to

keep her post on the outer rim of the group.

With his trusty staff, Isaac took his time inspecting each sheep, goat, and cow under his charge. The group had multiplied and appeared healthy in the fresh season of life. His chest should have swelled with pride, but one trip to his father's tent deflated him like an empty wine sack. The flocks were not the only ones welcoming new life. Keturah's growing midsection had become undeniable. Abraham would soon be expanding his tent for the first time in nearly forty years.

Isaac should have been happy for his father. After all, Elohim had promised to make Abraham and Sarah the first of many. Isaac shook his head. He was supposed to be the beginning of that promise, not the end.

Visions of his half-brother, Ishmael, filled his thoughts. He looked to the clear sky. The time had come. He had finally made his decision. The hard part was going to be telling his father.

That night, Isaac sat in Abraham's tent while Keturah's servants prepared a meal of lentil stew with fresh vegetables and platters of fruits. The room was quiet as those gathered ate in peace.

Isaac tried to keep his eyes focused on his food, but he often found them drifting toward Keturah's stomach. He didn't know how much longer until she held her new bundle, but if women were anything like sheep it wouldn't be long.

When she caught his gaze, he cleared his throat and turned his attention to Abraham. "Father, I have need to speak with you."

Abraham put down his bowl and waved his hand. "Speak on, my son."

Isaac stirred his stew with the last piece of bread. "I've thought and prayed about my decision and I feel it's time for me to move south."

Keturah's attention darted toward Abraham.

The old man pulled his long, gray beard. "You're sure?"

"With your growing family," he nodded toward Keturah, "you'll need the room."

"You've already moved to sleeping with the herdsmen out in the fields. Why must you move further?"

"I'm nearing forty and have no claim of my own. I've managed your shepherds for years; I think I can make a living being my own manager."

"And you've prayed over this decision?"

Isaac nodded. He had prayed, but his father's God had not answered. "I request my own flocks and my mother's tent."

He flinched and stiffened his back. "Your mother's tent?"

"It's all I have left of her."

Abraham thought for several moments. "Very well. As I can't seem to talk you into staying, I suppose we should do everything to help you start your new life out right." He rubbed his beard free of crumbs. "Choose of the herdsmen a companion and take your flocks and his share with you. I will see to it you are supplied with your mother's tent and any of her possessions with which I am willing to part."

Isaac sighed with relief. He hoped for this outcome and had already chosen the man whom he wanted to go with him. "I'm honored by your assistance. I choose Jedidiah to accompany me."

"A fine choice. When will you want to leave?"

"As soon as arrangements can be made. The flocks will need to move soon anyway. All have finished lambing, and the weather is favorable for the move. I figure it's as good a time as any." He leaned closer as if to share a secret. "We don't want a repeat of the incident with Lot."

Abraham's eyes misted over as if he were looking back into the past. "No. We don't." He shook his head. "I see you've put a great deal of thought into this."

"Then the matter is settled?"

He nodded. "May you be blessed, my son."

Isaac scooped the rest of his stew onto the bite of bread and popped it into his mouth.

After the evening meal, Isaac retreated to the fields to find Jedidiah. The fellow shepherd was gathering the flocks in closer for the night. Isaac called for Tira to herd the stragglers.

"So, how did the talk go?" Jedidiah kept his sights on the animals.

"*Abba* has agreed to allow me leave."

"That's wonderful." He beamed. "I'm glad to hear it, though you'll be missed greatly."

"Well, at least you won't miss my leadership."

He scrunched his forehead. "I don't understand."

"You're coming with me."

Jedidiah let his mouth hang slack. "I don't know what to say."

"Say you'll join me."

He nodded and put his hand on Isaac's shoulder. "Obviously I'll join you. It would be a great honor."

"I was hoping you'd find the arrangement agreeable." Isaac looked to the flocks. "We will begin our preparations at first light. I'd like to leave while the season is still favorable."

"Do you know where we are heading?"

"South. To Beerlahairoi."

Jedidiah turned away. "Where Hagar and Ishmael live?"

"I'm hoping to make contact with my brother." He watched for a reaction from his brother of the field.

Jedidiah stood still, as if frozen in concentrated thought.

"After we are settled of course." Isaac puffed his chest slightly. "The wellbeing of the flocks will come first."

"Good to hear." Jedidiah turned slightly and smiled.

"Well, I have some things to attend to in my father's tent before I take my watch." He patted his dog's head. "I'll see you then."

Jedidiah nodded.

Isaac walked back to Abraham's tent bathing in the cool air of the fields of Hebron and the bright moon above. He wasn't sure how many nights he would remain in the area before all necessary preparations could be made for his departure.

The massive flocks had been brought close so the shepherds could keep a better eye on them. Oil lamps in all the tents of Abraham's caravan were being lowered for the night. Isaac returned to his father's tent to find Abraham and Keturah had already retired into their back room.

He moved silently to the storage area to rummage through his mother's belongings. Sarah had left many packs behind when she departed the living world. Abraham had regifted many of her belongings to his new wife. Much to the churning of Isaac's stomach, his mother's clothes and prized jewelry hung on Keturah. Though he couldn't fault the old man because possessions were highly favored and hard to come by.

One bag held a few of Sarah's older garments. Another contained some loose gems and pieces of silver. He discovered a third held the carefully wrapped goatskin of her tent. He took stock of what was available to discuss with his father what he would be allowed to take. Any extra provisions would be helpful in starting his new life.

Of course, the one thing that would be helpful, Abraham had not taken the opportunity to bring up. A wife. Someone with which to share his new life.

Isaac sighed and retied the packs. Maybe the God who saw Hagar would also see him in Beerlahairoi.

Chapter 5

"So [Hagar] called the name of the LORD who spoke to her, 'You are a God of seeing,' for she said, 'Truly here I have seen him who looks after me.' "
-Genesis 16:13

Aleppo, 2025 B.C.
Rebekah

Rebekah watched the group of men set up the tents near a pomegranate grove. The sweet scent of their buds told her the season of new life had firmly planted its hold on the earth. Her thoughts should have been turning to an upcoming trip to the tablelands. Instead, she wondered how much longer she would ride atop a camel.

Eliezer sat a few handbreadths away instructing the four guards.

The largest man in the group held a tent flap in place. Rebekah remembered Eliezer had introduced him as Layth. He seemed to be sort of the leader of the guard. She wasn't sure if it had anything to do with his size or age or both.

Rebekah took in the dark skin, dark eyes, and large muscles of the broad man. His face was almost light with work. His eyes still kept to the surroundings, but he seemed to enjoy his hands being busy. His face was slightly rounded like a child, but one glimpse at the rest of him proved otherwise. He was so massive she was sure he could rip apart a wolf with his bare hands.

Her gaze shifted to the man driving a peg into the sand. Taj. He wasn't as muscular as his fellow servant, but his skin was just as toasted by work in the sun. She'd seen him carving as they sat around the fire at night. The calluses on his hands were strong indicators of a hard-working man.

The third guard, Dov, brushed his hands free of sand. He was large enough to be a threatening presence, but his demeanor was as calm as a flowing river.

Her eyes found the last man adjusting one of the center tent poles. Meir. He seemed the youngest of the four men, but by no means a child. His frame was sturdy and strong. His skin was not as dark, giving more evidence that he had not spent as long under the sun as the others.

Eliezer caught her stare and made his way over to her. "The tents should be ready soon." He looked to the men. "I hope you find your guard suitable. They are all good men," he assured her. "Layth and Taj were born into Master Abraham's service. Dov and Meir have been with us since they were children."

"I've never understood children servants."

Eliezer's eyes darkened. "Not all homes are as kind as yours. Knowing only some details of their lives, they have fared much better under the hand of my master."

"And you? Were you born or bought?"

He smiled. "Ah, that is a story for another night."

"Then what of tonight's story?"

He pulled at his beard. "I'd like to tell you of Isaac's brother."

"Brother?" Her eyes widened. "I didn't realize he had siblings."

"They share Abraham as their father, but they do not come from the same mother's womb."

"Does he live with Isaac and Abraham?"

Eliezer rose. "Let's gather some wood for the fire, and I'll tell you about him."

Rebekah stood and scouted for sticks as she listened.

"Master Abraham's wife, Sarah, had a handmaid named Hagar. She was a beautiful Egyptian woman; a gift from Pharaoh himself." He picked up a dry branch. "After ten years of living in the land of Canaan, Sarah had not been able to give Abraham a child. So, she offered her handmaid to him as a concubine."

A tremor ran down Rebekah's spine as she reached for a few twigs. "I don't care much for that practice."

"I am of a like mind. As Elohim created Eve for

Adam and blessed their union, I too believe it should be with us. But sadly, we do not always follow the original plan."

"And Abraham? He doesn't agree with his Elohim's plan?"

Eliezer adjusted the bundle in his arm. "I think Sarah had much more to do with his shifting opinion than his own desire." He smiled, then the simple smile faded. "Unfortunately, you won't have the opportunity to meet Sarah. But had you, you would understand. She was a ferocious person. Often seeming far larger than the petite package of flesh she was wrapped in."

"She is no longer?"

He shook his head. "I'm afraid not. She died a few years ago." He opened his mouth to speak, but shut it slowly and shook his head again. "I fear Isaac didn't take the loss well."

Her heart squeezed thinking of the absence of her father. Even though they hadn't met yet, she understood her betrothed even if only in empathy.

"But this is Hagar's story."

She scrunched her brow. "I thought you said it was Ishmael's?"

"But his story starts with hers." He added his bundle to the growing stack beside the fire Dov was working on starting. "So, at Sarah's insistence, Abraham took Hagar as a concubine and went in unto her. She conceived right away."

"I bet he was happy."

Eliezer sat down. "He was, but Sarah was not."

Rebekah pulled at her fingers. "I thought you said Sarah was the one who pushed for it to be so."

His smile reached up into his eyes. "She was. But sometimes when we finally get what we want, we find out it's not really what we wanted after all."

Rebekah knelt beside him. Her own struggles with desire and uncertainty warred inside her.

"When Hagar discovered she carried Abraham's seed, she became very proud in Sarah's sight. Poor Sarah spent months face to face with the consequences of her own choices."

"What did she do?"

"She attempted to blame Abraham at first, but he wouldn't hear any of it. He told her that Hagar was her property to do with what she pleased."

"She didn't hurt her, did she?"

"No, but she didn't treat her as kind as she had before. Finally, Hagar couldn't take anymore and decided to leave."

"Where did she go?"

"She was headed for home back in Egypt, but she didn't make it."

Rebekah tilted her head.

"A divine messenger found her by a spring in Shur. He called her by name and asked where she was going and from where she had come." He leaned back. "She told the messenger that she was running away from her mistress, and he told her to return."

"Go back? Why would she return if she were being mistreated?"

"The messenger instructed her to submit to her mistress and that her seed would be multiplied. He also told her that she was carrying a son and to name him Ishmael because her affliction had been heard."

"It must be hard to submit to someone who dislikes you."

"Submission is not always easy, but it is oftentimes required. In doing so, Hagar learned that by submitting to her mistress, she was really submitting to the One Who saw her. That is why she called Elohim's name El Roi, the God Who Sees, because she saw the One Who saw her. She named the place where she was Beerlahairoi, which means the well of the Living One Who Sees me."

"So, Hagar returned to Sarah?"

"She did and she bore a son and called his name Ishmael as she had been told. Regrettably, that didn't mean things were easy for her."

"No?"

"Sometime later, when Sarah did bear Isaac and they were celebrating his weaning, Ishmael made fun of his younger brother. He found the display of a mother chewing up food and spitting it into the younger boy's mouth quite funny. Sarah didn't appreciate his humor and asked Abraham to send them away."

"Did he?"

"I'm afraid so. He gave them provisions and sent them on their way. They wandered in the wilderness of Beersheba attempting to reach Egypt again. That was until their provisions dried up. When Ishmael couldn't walk any further, Hagar hid him under some brush and walked away. She cried out to El Roi, pleading to Him that she wouldn't have to watch her son die."

"Did El Roi see her again?"

"He did. Another divine messenger arrived to tell Hagar not to worry about Ishmael and reminded her of the promise that had been made concerning him becoming a great nation. Then he showed her a well where she was able to refill their waterskins and give a drink to Ishmael."

"Did they return to Abraham again?"

"No. We were told they journeyed further south to live in the wilderness of Paran."

Rebekah noticed the others had gathered around to hear the rest of the story. They were just as interested. She wondered about Elohim and how different He seemed compared to other gods. She couldn't think of any other god who had listened to the cries of a concubine and her illegitimate son, much less answered those cries with promises of provision and power.

Chapter 6

*"[Ishmael] lived in the wilderness of Paran, and his
mother took a wife for him from the land of Egypt."
-Genesis 21:21*

Kadesh, 2025 B.C.
Isaac

Isaac and Jedidiah came upon the gates of Kadesh.

"Are you sure you want to do this?" Jedidiah didn't
take his eyes off the path in front of them. "I mean, it
has been a long time since you've seen one another.
What if Ishmael doesn't welcome you?"

"We've been settled in Beerlahairoi for over a year
now. I've been putting off this trip long enough. It's
time I face what I came south to do. If I fail, I will at
least know that I tried my best." He entered the city.

After several inquiries in the market, they were
pointed in the direction of Ishmael's home.

When they came upon the gates of a large villa, a
woman raised her hand over her brown eyes against the

bright sun.

"Ahh, the favored son approaches." The woman came near the entrance.

Isaac recognized Hagar at once. Though several decades had passed, her beauty had not been marred by time's hands.

"What do we owe the honor of a visit from the favored son of Abraham?" Her tone held an air of smugness.

He shook off her haughtiness. "I wish to speak to my brother."

"He's a very popular man." Her eyes danced with arrogance. "I don't know if he'd have time to grant an audience with you."

"Please. I just want to talk to him."

Her gaze appraised him and then Jedidiah. "Stay here. I will see if he is available."

"Thank you."

She turned and almost floated away toward the grand house.

The day slipped by as the two men waited at the gate. Isaac kept an eye on the sun's track across the sky. As it melted beyond the city walls, he was ready to give up for the day. He stood and motioned for Jedidiah to follow.

The sound of movement from behind grabbed their attention.

Hagar had returned. She unlocked the gate and held it open. "Ishmael will see you, but only briefly. As

I said, he is very busy."

"I'll be brief." Isaac slipped in the narrow opening. Jedidiah moved to follow.

Hagar put up a hand to the shepherd and wrinkled her nose. "Your companion can wait out here."

Isaac nodded to him. "I won't be long."

Jedidiah shrugged and stepped back.

Hagar locked the gate and waved toward the villa. "This way."

Isaac followed her lead through the massive garden courtyard and into the house. The grand structure was immaculately kept with servants hurrying in all directions. Furniture of all kinds filled the open areas and mosaics covered floors and walls. Isaac swallowed hard. What business did he have seeking out his brother who was obviously better off without him in his life?

As they approached a back room, two guards stood outside flanking the doorway. Isaac took note of their immense frames and unpleasant demeanor assessing him as he passed them and paused at the entryway.

Inside the room, Ishmael stood beside a low table. Piles of scrolls were scattered on top, and he held one in his hands studying its contents.

Isaac immediately noticed the similarities they shared with their father. A strong jawline, broad shoulders, and sparkling eyes all reminded him of Abraham. Ishmael's skin tone contained much more of the rich depth of his mother's Egyptian heritage, and he held some of her attractiveness in the rest of his face.

With a bow, Hagar announced, "May I present Abraham's son, Isaac."

At the name, Ishmael's attention abruptly turned toward them.

The clear look of shock on Ishmael's face caused Isaac to doubt Hagar had told Ishmael of his presence at their gate for most of the day. Some emotion teetering between confusion and indecision crossed Ishmael's face before he regained his composure. "Come in, come in." He waved.

Isaac bowed and then took a few steps deeper into the room.

Hagar fluttered toward her son and kissed him on both cheeks.

Ishmael patted his mother's arm. "Thank you, *Ima.*"

She hung beside him.

Ishmael studied Isaac for several long moments.

Isaac started counting his heartbeats to keep from speaking out of turn.

When it seemed Ishmael had reached an internal decision, he looked down at his mother and caught her gaze. "I'd like a private word with my brother, if you don't mind."

Her face twisted into a pout. "I am simply looking out for your best interest."

"I'm sure my brother has no ill intentions." He looked at Isaac.

Isaac lifted empty palms and shook his head.

"There, you see. I will be fine."

"Well, there are guards within listening distance should you need them."

Ishmael attempted a smile. "Thank you, *Ima*."

Hagar hesitated for a moment before she left the room.

Ishmael stared at Isaac for another long stretch of heartbeats.

Dryness crept up the back of Isaac's throat causing him to cough to clear it.

"Ahh, forgive me." He waved to a pile of pillows. "Please make yourself comfortable. Would you care for something to drink? I can have something brought in."

"I'm well." Even though his parched throat felt like he had licked a sand dune, Isaac waved off the offer. "I won't take up your time with hospitalities. I only ask for a few moments to talk with you."

"Of course." He sat across from him. "Speak on."

"I seek you out not to ask anything of you, but merely to… well…seek you."

Ishmael's eyes sparkled as he stared at him for another long moment. "Forgive my gaze, but I was just thinking how much you grew up to look like *Abba*."

"I was just thinking the same thing about you."

"Do you think?" He rubbed his bearded chin. "*Ima* always said so. Of course, you resemble him much more than I. And your *ima*. I see her in you too."

At the mention of his mother, Isaac's heart thudded. Her beautiful face lit his vision and the pain of loss threatened to drag him under its dark grip.

After a few moments of wrestling with his emotions, Isaac looked up to see his brother watching him. He cleared his throat and admitted, "I fear I'm not much like her at all."

"Ahh, but you are." He lifted a hand and curled it into a tight fist in front of himself. "I see her fire in your face. She is a strong woman."

"She was."

Understanding struck like lightning across Ishmael's face as he relaxed. "What happened?"

"It's been a few years now." He swallowed past the rising lump in his throat. "She became very ill and…"

"I see." His gaze dropped to the floor. "I'm sorry for your loss."

"Thank you." He breathed through the mounting waves of emotion. "*Abba* remarried and has started another family."

"You don't say." He leaned back; amusement clear on his face. "Old Abraham fathering more children?"

"Soon after I settled in Beerlahairoi, I received word they had welcomed a son. They call him Zimran."

Ishmael's shoulders fell slightly. "*Abba* isn't here with you?"

Isaac shook his head. "He and his new wife, Keturah, settled in Hebron. When I realized they would be starting a family, I decided to move south. I remembered the story of your mother and thought Beerlahairoi would be a nice place to raise my flocks."

Ishmael's bushy brows lifted. "Are you seeking the One Who Sees?"

The unanswering silence from his father's God mocked him. "Perhaps."

"Then there is no better place to hear from El Roi than in Beerlahairoi."

Isaac looked to the tiled floor.

"Speaking of families."

His attention came up.

"I've got twelve sons of my own." He beamed with pride.

"Twelve? How truly blessed you are."

"It's true. They have settled from Havilah to Shur and become great leaders."

"El Roi has blessed you."

"And what of you? How many sons do you have?"

Isaac's countenance fell. "None."

"Daughters?"

He leaned forward to drape his hands over his knees. "I don't even have a wife." Isaac thought about all the women he had encountered since moving south. Though they were all beautiful and many willing to be wife to the son of wealthy Abraham, Isaac held onto hope that his father would remember his duty in choosing a bride for him.

"I see." Ishmael pulled at his dark beard. "I thought

Abba was told you'd be the start of a great nation."

"I thought so too."

Silence hung between the brothers as each searched for their next words.

"*Ima* selected the most beautiful Egyptian woman for me." Ishmael's face brightened. "She is out today, but perhaps the next time you visit you can meet her."

"I'd like that."

Ishmael reached over and gave Isaac's shoulder a firm squeeze.

The gesture was warm and reassuring as Isaac had wished a touch from an older brother would be.

"I'm sure *Abba* will find you an equal beauty when he feels the time is right."

He nodded. If forty years hadn't produced the right time, what hope did he have for the future? Abraham wasn't going to live forever and time waited for no one. He rose slowly. "I suppose I should be going. I don't want to keep you from your work."

Ishmael stood. "But you just arrived." His sable eyes penetrated Isaac's.

"I will visit again. If I'm welcomed?"

Ishmael threw his massive arms around Isaac. "Always, brother."

He bowed deeply and turned to leave the room. When he passed the guards, a movement in his side vision caught his attention.

Hagar stood a very short distance from the doorway. Her haughty eyes and smug smile told him she had heard every word of the supposedly private conversation.

"Hail the favored son of Abraham." She bowed far deeper than she had to.

Isaac nodded a proper bow and saw himself out the front door, through the lavish garden, and to the courtyard gate.

When the metal lock clicked behind him, he hurried toward the city gate without a backward glance.

"Wait for me." Jedidiah scurried after him.

Isaac slowed his pace. "Apologies."

"I take it the talk didn't go so well?"

"The talk went great." He shrugged. "I'm not sure what I expected. Ishmael's doing well. He's got twelve sons who are rulers. He lives in a grand villa with armed guards. His mother is…alive."

"Then why does your face appear as if his guards whipped you?"

He hesitated. "He's got everything I was supposed to have."

"So, you're jealous?"

Mixed ideas and emotions contorted their way through his mind and body. "I don't know. A little. I mean, I'm happy that he is well and prosperous. I just wish…"

"That you had some of that prosperity too?"

Isaac stopped and glanced over his shoulder. The large villa was still in view. "It's not even so much the physical prosperity."

"So, the family then?"

He nodded and returned his focus to the city's exit.

Isaac put a hand up to shield his eyes from the blazing sun radiating down on him in the open field. A figure approached from the north. Before the form became clear, Isaac knew who it was from the old man's familiar gait.

"Greetings, Eliezer." He waved as he came near.

The old servant nodded. "Greetings, Isaac. I trust this day finds you well."

"As well as any other." His eyes scanned the herds around him. "What news have you?"

"I come bearing a message from your father."

At the mention of his father, Isaac set his gaze back on him. "Oh?"

"Aren't you going to invite an old man to sit in the shade?"

Isaac shook his head. "My apologies. Of course. Right this way." He led Eliezer to his tent which he had set up and left the sides open. The goatskin flapped in the breeze and provided ample shade from the heat of the day.

The servant sat on a worn-out pillow, adjusting his old frame to a comfortable position.

Isaac knelt beside him. "Water?" He offered him a waterskin.

"Thank you." He took a long drink before handing the pouch back.

Isaac took a sip and set the skin aside. "Now then, what word do you bring from my *abba*?"

"It seems the events of the last two years have caused your father great concern."

"Is he well?"

"Quite well. He and Keturah are happy together. Zimran has seen his first year and will soon be an older brother."

Isaac's brows lifted.

"Yes, it seems your father will be welcoming another addition."

He swallowed hard, pushing the rise of emotions down with a lump. "Thank you for bringing this word."

"Oh, that's not what I came to tell you."

"No?"

He shook his head. "Master Abraham's second child has brought his thoughts to you. When you left, he was so busy with his new life that it took a while before he realized how much your absence affected him."

Isaac wanted to chuckle. What effect would his lack of presence have on a man well into his second life?

"But with time and seasons of life changing, he's come to realize his lack concerning you."

He held his breath.

"He's charged me with finding you a wife."

The words were too wonderful to believe. A wife? Now? Isaac shook his shock away. "From Canaan?"

"No." Eliezer leaned back; his neck almost disappeared behind the curtain of his thick beard. "It seems Master Abraham finds them...unsuitable for you."

"I see."

"No, I am to take a caravan all the way back to Padanaram, to the place of his family to find your bride."

"Padanaram? That's a very long journey." He quickly calculated the distance. "More than a full moon's cycle just to get there and another to return."

"Without complications."

His eyes widened. He had merely accounted for a smooth journey.

Eliezer gazed toward the open area. "The added potential for impassable weather, lurking danger, or any number of other hazards would only add to the length of our return. And, of course, that's all dependent upon the fact that I am successful in my charge to begin with."

"You're not sure if you will be?"

"Only Elohim knows." He set his eyes back on Isaac. "I came to tell you so that you could prepare for her arrival."

Isaac's chest felt heavy. Elohim hadn't been much help to him so far. How could he trust a God who only spoke to one man to find him a bride?

Chapter 7

"Abraham answered and said, "Behold, I have undertaken to speak to the Lord, I who am but dust and ashes.' "
-Genesis 18:27

Ebla, 2025 B.C.
Rebekah

Rebekah walked among the market streets of the fortress city of Ebla. Hadiya flanked her on one side with Layth and Taj following close behind. The others had split into a second group with Eliezer to find an Inn for the night.

Stretching her legs and enjoying the sights of a city were a much-needed reprieve from riding a camel and staring off into the endless horizon with only her thoughts to keep her entertained between Eliezer's stories. Rebekah had lost count of how many cities they had passed and didn't know how many more would have to be crossed before her journey would end.

Hadiya paused at a fruit stand to examine a choice fig. "Are you excited about meeting your betrothed soon?"

Flutters danced in Rebekah's stomach. "I don't know if I would use exactly that word."

Hadiya set the fig down and picked up a pomegranate. Lifting it to her nose, she inhaled its sweet scent. "If I were you, I'd be excited to meet a man who fetched me from across the world."

Rebekah's mouth twisted sideways. "He didn't fetch me, his *abba* did. I've never even met my Great *Dod* Abraham, much less his son. What guarantee do I have that they are good people?"

Hadiya returned the fruit to its place on the stand with a shrug. "Eliezer seems caring enough. Perhaps you should take that as a good sign."

Signs. Rebekah was sick of signs. Vague pictures in dreams. Strange servants making pacts with unseen deities. She needed someone to just tell her the straight truth. "Perhaps."

Eliezer walked up to them. "We have secured lodging for tonight."

"I'm glad." Rebekah took a deep breath. "It truly wasn't necessary. I'm used to sleeping in tents for long stretches."

"The others are as well, but it is nice to enjoy a strong roof over one's head every once in a while."

Rebekah reached for a fig and gave it a squeeze. Her nearly empty money pouch hit against her body with the movement reminding her of her lack of funds. She didn't have the chance to take her flock to market before they left. With a sigh, she returned the delicious-looking fruit.

Eliezer picked up the same fig and handed it to her. "Whatever you desire, simply ask."

Rebekah turned the fruit in her hand. "I don't have much money."

"Your funds are not necessary."

She looked to the merchant and back to the servant. "I don't understand."

"Anything you need will be purchased with Master Abraham's funds." He reached into his cloak and produced a small sliver of silver and handed it to the man. "My good merchant, would you mind allowing me the use of your scale?"

The man looked Eliezer up and down. "For what purpose? My scale is fairly balanced."

"I'm sure it is." He waved off the man's concern. "That's why I have need of it."

With suspicious glances, he moved his scale toward Eliezer.

"My dear, I wish to show you more about the God I follow." He cleared the two plates of debris and stacked good fruit on one side and over-ripened ones on the other. "Your belief system tells you that your deeds and accomplishments in this life will provide lasting fame. After your death, one must make a difficult journey to the Netherworld. Upon arrival there, they take account of your status on earth, how your body had been prepared, and how many children you were able to produce."

The scales balanced as he continued stacking fruits on each side.

"No matter what you do, it has only minimal effect on the life to come."

She shrugged. The afterlife was not one of her favorite ideas to dwell on. She had to focus too much on staying alive in the present to concern herself with what lay ahead of her after this life ended.

"Well, Elohim isn't like that."

"He doesn't take account of your life?"

"He does. In a different way." He waved to the bad fruit. "If He had scales, all your deeds would be as these unpleasant selections." He removed all the good fruit from the other side and replaced it with his heavy money pouch. "And all His would be as the precious things this world can contain. No matter what you did, your deeds would never be able to compare to His."

"It seems impossible to please a god like that."

"Ahh." He held up a finger. "Exactly. So, what is one to do?"

She exchanged an uncertain glance with the merchant.

"What Elohim does is not like this scale at all." He stretched. "My good merchant, could you write me a bill for several pieces of your finest fruit?"

The man's attention fell to the large money pouch

and then back to the man. He tilted his head to one side and held his mouth open.

"Indulge an old servant."

The man shrugged with a deep huff. He took out a scrap of parchment and stylus to write up a simple bill.

"Make it out in Rebekah's name."

Rebekah let her shoulders drop. "But I told you, I don't have any—"

Eliezer held up a hand to her. "Just wait."

The merchant finished and handed the parchment to Rebekah.

Her eyes studied the price she couldn't afford. Then she looked to Eliezer. "Now what?"

"This is Elohim." He held out his hand. "Give me your bill."

She tentatively slipped the document into his waiting hand.

Eliezer snatched his pouch from the scale and paid the amount listed. Then he handed the merchant the bill.

The man scribbled across the charge and handed the parchment back to Rebekah.

Her eyes squinted at the rough letters. "Fully paid." She looked up at Eliezer.

"And so it is with Elohim. You see, when we have faith in Him, that act is credited to our account as righteousness. When He forgives the debt against us, it is fully paid because true forgiveness is canceling a debt that was rightfully owed."

Rebekah's gaze fell back to the parchment. She studied the words again trying to make sense of the lesson.

"I think it's time I tell you about your cousin Lot. But first," he handed her an empty sack, "redeem your purchase."

Rebekah settled next to Deborah while Hadiya passed around the platters of food the Innkeeper had provided them. She pulled out her overflowing bag of fruit and sat it among the offerings.

Eliezer waited until all were settled in the large room before offering a simple prayer to Elohim.

When he was through, Rebekah took a sip of fresh water and picked from the platter of sheep cheese.

Eliezer looked at Rebekah. "You know of Lot, yes?"

She nodded. "Only that he was the son of my Great *Dod* Haran who died in Ur." She thought back to the fragments of conversations she had heard. "When Abraham left, he took Lot with him."

"Yes, he took Lot as a son." Eliezer passed a tray of lamb meat to Taj. "They traveled through Canaan together looking for land. Due to the size of their flocks, I'm afraid they ended up having to part ways."

"So, Lot doesn't live with Abraham anymore?"

He shook his head solemnly. "Lot chose a dark path."

Rebekah chewed on her choice fig.

"Lot's eyes and heart led him to a city filled with much evil called Sodom." He settled in deeper on his mound of pillows. "Once, when Abraham was nearing one hundred years old, three men came to visit him, but these were no ordinary men."

"Who were they?"

"Master Abraham believed that two of them were messengers sent from Elohim."

"And the third?"

"Elohim Himself, wrapped in flesh. Master Abraham called Him, Adonai."

Rebekah chewed slower considering what a meeting with the divine would have been like.

"Master Abraham ordered Sarah to prepare them a meal. They ate and the beings revealed wondrous things to Abraham, but they also delivered a grave warning. Because of the wickedness in Sodom and the neighboring city of Gomorrah, Adonai was going to destroy them. In fact, the two messengers were on their way to destroy the cities that very day."

"Did Abraham try to stop them?"

"He tried. He bartered with Adonai to stay His judgment if even a few righteous could be found among the wicked. Abraham knew that Lot, his wife, daughters, and sons-in-law all lived in Sodom."

"Did it work?"

He shook his head. "Not even Lot and his family could be counted among the righteous. Adonai couldn't even find one."

"How could that be? If Lot went with Abraham out of Haran, surely he believed in Elohim?"

"It seemed so, but when Lot moved his family to Sodom the wickedness of that city was so great that it revealed the true nature of Lot's heart."

Her lips parted as she forgot about her fig.

"The two messengers went to Sodom and found Lot sitting at the gate. He rose to meet them and brought them into his house. They told him they wanted to stay in the center of town, but Lot knew how dangerous it would be for them if they did. The men of the city would seek them for personal pleasure because they were not of this world."

"Did they stay with Lot?"

"Lot was able to sway them, but the men of the city found out about the visitors and surrounded the house calling for them to be handed over." He looked down and shook his head. "Lot even offered his own betrothed daughters who had not yet lain with their own husbands as tribute instead of the visitors."

Rebekah felt heat course through her veins. "How dare he!"

"The men of Sodom refused the offer and attempted to break down the door. Thankfully, the messengers were able to strike the men with blindness in order to get Lot and his family out. They asked if he had any other kin in the city. Lot told them about his sons-in-law, but when they attempted to rescue them, the men thought he was joking about the coming judgment."

"They wouldn't leave?"

"They didn't believe him." He folded his hands over his full stomach. "When morning came, the messengers told Lot it was time to leave. He hesitated, so the messengers forced them outside the city. They told them to flee and not to look back."

Rebekah remembered the last glance she had of her home on the day she left. "Just leave their home without a backward glance?"

Eliezer nodded. "The messengers told them to run toward the hills, but Lot asked to go to Zoar instead. Once they were close to the nearby city, Adonai rained fire from the sky on Sodom and Gomorrah, but…"

Rebekah waited.

The old servant kept his gaze down.

"But?"

"Lot's wife looked back." He looked up to meet her eyes.

She covered a gasp. "What happened to her?"

"Adonai turned her into a pillar of salt. Lot fled with his two daughters to the hills because he thought Adonai was going to continue His judgment on the rest of the world. The three of them remained hidden away in a cave."

"That's awful."

His face contorted into a pained expression. "I'm afraid that's not the end of the story."

"No?" She took a sip of water from the pouch she was passed.

He shook his head and adjusted his body as if the thought of what he had to say made him physically uncomfortable. "They believed the entire world had been destroyed along with all the people in it. So, the two daughters of Lot made their father drunk with wine and laid with him so they could have his offspring."

Rebekah spit out the water in her mouth. "Why?"

"With the grand scale of the destruction they had witnessed, they truly believed the end of all other men had come. As I said, living in Sodom revealed the real Lot. He had followed Abraham, but he did not follow Elohim."

Rebekah wiped away the drops of water on her chin. She stared at the group who continued eating in silence. She had heard some high tales of flesh, but hearing what her cousins did to their father turned her stomach. How desperate and how far they must have been persuaded away from Elohim's path to make such choices.

Chapter 8

"As for Ishmael, I have heard you; behold, I have blessed him and will make him fruitful and multiply him greatly. He shall father twelve princes, and I will make him into a great nation."
-Genesis 17:20

Kadesh, 2025 B.C.
Isaac

Isaac drove his large group of animals through the crowded streets of Kadesh with Jedidiah. It had only been a few weeks since Isaac reconnected with Ishmael, but somehow the city felt just as looming as his first visit. This was Isaac's chance to prove himself a good trader in the market.

Jedidiah pushed the goats closer. "All I'm saying is to give your father a chance. If he believes sending Eliezer to Haran will secure you the best wife, then let him. What's the worst that could happen? A wife is a wife no matter where she comes from."

"Because, in a normal betrothal, the bridegroom usually at least knows the family. I've never met that side of *Abba's* family. I don't know them at all. What if they worship worse gods than those in Canaan?"

Jedidiah's steps halted. "No one worships worse gods than those found in Canaan."

Isaac rolled his eyes. "You know what I mean. *Abba* says he separated from them all those years ago because they didn't believe he heard from Elohim. That means they must follow something else. Even Great *Abba* Terah carved and sold idols."

The hired hand leaned on his staff. "Is that what this is really about?"

Isaac's legs tensed. Jedidiah had always been good at reading his internal struggles. "What's that supposed to mean?"

He shrugged. "We've been living in Beerlahairoi for over two years, and I've never seen you once offer a sacrifice as your father used to."

Isaac felt as if a boulder had been dropped into his stomach. "I guess I haven't."

"There, you see. So, what is the real issue?"

He rubbed the back of his neck. "I don't know."

"Well," Jedidiah pushed off his staff, "you better figure it out. Eliezer will return at some point with your bride whether you're ready or not."

The men pressed deeper into the city trying to locate the portion of the market reserved for animals.

As Isaac passed the clothing stalls, he took note of

the beautiful selections of fine clothes. He wondered what sort of dress his far-fetched bride would wear and how comfortable she would be in clothing worn by a shepherd's wife.

The women of the city loitered in the streets. Their bright colors and adorned faces called out to every eye to look upon them. Giggles and high-pitched laughter filled the air around Isaac. It was a foreign sound and one much different from the bleating of sheep and goats and barking dogs to which he'd grown accustomed.

As he passed, the women turned their noses up with looks of clear disgust.

Isaac looked down at his muddy mantle. The thought to clean up and look presentable for the market had not occurred to him before that moment.

They searched his appearance and whispered to each other. Some pulled their material up around their faces as if to keep his smell away from their delicate noses.

His pace quickened to be rid of their haughty glances.

At the end of the dusty road, the area opened to a large animal market filled with the sights and smells of livestock. This was far more familiar. Isaac had traveled to the market with his father in other cities on a number of occasions. He wasn't a bad barterer and his father often allowed him to take the lead on deals.

"Isaac?" a deep voice called from somewhere over

the bleating of sheep.

Isaac turned to search out the seeker.

Ishmael came close and greeted them. "It's good to see you back in Kadesh so soon."

"It is good to see you as well, brother. Though I hadn't planned a visit today."

"Then it's lucky for me that I came to the market this day." He turned toward the other man. "And who do we have here?"

"This is Jedidiah," Isaac explained. "My fellow shepherd and friend."

Ishmael bowed. "A pleasure."

Jedidiah returned the greeting.

Ishmael's gaze took in the massive herds behind them. "I see you have business to take care of."

Isaac nodded. "My flocks have grown large. I wanted to try my hand at your city's fair market."

A broad smile creased his face. "You sound so much like *Abba*." He chuckled. "Tell me, what is it you are looking to sell?"

"I breed sheep, goats, and cattle, but my specialty is a breed of dog from *Abba's* family."

"You breed Kangals?"

"He's the best breeder around." Jedidiah punched Isaac's shoulder. "His dogs are the finest. Much hardier than the Canaan breed."

Ishmael looked to the other shepherd and then back to his brother. "Is this true?"

He shrugged. "I enjoy the dogs, so I tend to spend

time with them. Maybe more than I should."

"Are you selling any today?"

He shook his head. "My best female is pregnant and will have a litter in the coming months, but I sold most of my last two litters before leaving home."

"Shame." He pressed his lips into a tight grimace. "Having a dog around might not be a bad idea."

"I could certainly send word when the pups are weaned."

A smile eased his constricted lips. "See to it that you do. I'd be proud to own a fine dog from my brother."

Isaac felt a warmth spread through him. The sibling connection didn't seem lost on the son who had been exiled.

Ishmael folded his arms and pulled at his chin. "Now, if you were to ask my opinion, I'd send you down the way to Paebel. In all my dealings with him, I've known him to be an honest and fair man. Tell him I sent you and he'll be sure to give you a fair price for your animals."

"Truly?"

"What are brothers for?"

Isaac pondered the question. The life he'd known had been void of a blood brother. Ishmael was a foggy memory of his infancy. His fellow shepherds were hired hands of his father, but many of them were as close as a brother could get. Still, at the end of the day, their place in the family was one of employment that could be severed at any moment. Isaac longed for the closeness he felt when he was around Ishmael. Why hadn't he chosen to leave home sooner?

Chapter 9

"When Abram was ninety-nine years old the LORD appeared to Abram and said to him, 'I am God Almighty; walk before me, and be blameless, that I may make my covenant between me and you, and may multiply you greatly.'"
-Genesis 17:1-2

Hamath, 2025 B.C.
Rebekah

Rebekah awoke suddenly. Her breaths came short and shallow. Drops of sweat ran down her face.

From the still darkness she heard Hadiya whisper, "The dream again?"

Rebekah's voice was stuck in the dream world. She tried to reach up to wipe her face, but her arms wouldn't obey. She willed her limbs to move and her mouth to speak, but she felt as if she were stuck in a sand dune.

Hadiya's call came a little louder, "Rebekah?"

Whatever hold her dream had on her throat was finally released. "I'm well."

She felt something move next to her, then a hand wrapped around hers.

"You were restless again."

"I'm sorry I woke you."

"No need to apologize. You can't control them."

Hadiya's strong grip and soothing words set Rebekah firmly in the real world and eased her strained muscles. "If only I could." She wiped her face with her free hand and scooted closer to her handmaid.

"Was this one any different than the last?"

She shook her head, then realized Hadiya couldn't see her in the dark. "Not really. They are just getting more…"

"More?"

"Intense." She turned her head trying to find Hadiya's face in the darkness. "Do you believe I'm going mad?"

Hadiya squeezed her hand tighter. "Of course not. I believe you are the most stable woman I know."

"Then why do I keep having this same dream?"

"Maybe it truly is a sign. Like when you met Eliezer. You said the dream changed at the end before you met him. When you emptied the water into the trough, your reflection showed you with jewelry and a fine garment."

Rebekah reached up and fingered the clip-on nose ring Eliezer had put on her. Over the days of travel, she had grown accustomed to the bridal decoration. "So?"

"Well, maybe the dream growing stronger is a sign too?"

"For what?"

Hadiya released her grasp and moved her arm to hug Rebekah close. "I'm afraid, Mistress, you did not purchase a seer. I only know the future when it becomes the present."

Rebekah sighed.

"Maybe you should speak with Eliezer. He seems very wise."

The wrinkled face of the old servant appeared in Rebekah's thoughts. Eliezer had regaled them with stories every day of the trip. The men respected him in word and deed. "Perhaps."

"Rest now." Hadiya adjusted into a more comfortable spot. "The sun will be up before we know it."

She reached over and brushed Hadiya's hair. "I shall certainly try."

Rebekah watched the sunrise through the flapping tent opening. Hadiya had fallen asleep and remained that way through the last hours of night. Rebekah lay awake, mentally walking through every step of her dream and all the slight variations she could remember.

She came up as empty-handed as when she attempted to decipher its meaning.

With a long exhale, she stirred enough to wake Hadiya without startling her. "The sun has risen and so should we."

Hadiya lifted herself to a seated position. She stretched high into the air. "How did you sleep?"

Rebekah sat up, but kept her eyes from her handmaiden's gaze. "Well. Thank you."

"No more dream?"

She shook her head.

"Well, then I suppose we should get ready for the day." She stood and rolled up her sleeping mat.

Rebekah followed her lead.

Deborah ducked her head into the tent. "About time you two rise. These men have been waiting to break down your tent."

Rebekah gave Hadiya a sideways glance. "We will be out in a moment."

When the women were adequately dressed and packed, the men made quick work of disassembling their tent and loaded up the camels. They laid beautiful blankets on the camels' humps creating a soft place to ride.

Rebekah took Taj's offer of his hand to mount her camel. The beast rose under her as Eliezer took the group away from the city of Hamath and back toward the hot sands of the desert.

The four men circled the caravan with glances

always moving in every direction.

Rebekah leaned down to get Eliezer's attention. "Is their guard really necessary?"

"We carry very precious cargo."

The images of packs full of silver, jewels, and other materials sitting on her family's table filled her mind. "You unloaded much into the laps of my family. I don't see many other packs besides supplies. How much more precious cargo could you be carrying?"

Amusement lit Eliezer's eyes as a smile spread wide across his face. "I wasn't talking about the items measured by weights. I was referring to the one who will be used to measure out the stars."

She furrowed her brow as she thought on his words. "Measure the stars?"

He chuckled. "I told you of the day the three visitors came to my master, but what I didn't tell you is that they had a personal message for him before they told him what would happen to Sodom."

"What message?"

Eliezer adjusted the reigns of her camel. "While Sarah prepared food, the visitors inquired of where she was. Master Abraham told them she was in the tent. Then they told him that at the same time the following year, they would return to him and she would have a son." He lifted an eyebrow. "Of course, she was well past childbearing age because the way of women had ceased to be with her for a very long time. What Abraham didn't know was that Sarah was listening to them at the tent door."

"What did she do?"

"What any old woman would have done had someone told her she was going to be with child. She laughed."

Rebekah thought about it. "I suppose I would have laughed too."

"Well, the visitors heard her laughing and asked Abraham why she did. Then they affirmed that nothing was too difficult for Elohim and that Sarah would indeed have a son."

Her gaze lifted to the horizon.

"Sarah denied it then, but a few months later she couldn't deny their words."

"You mean…"

He nodded. "She did have a son the following year. Master Abraham was a hundred and Sarah was ninety when they became parents to Isaac."

"That's impossible."

"As Elohim said, 'Nothing is impossible with Him.' " He laughed. "Sometime before those events, Abraham had a vision from Elohim. One in which He promised to be Abraham's shield and very great reward. Abraham pleaded for the only thing he lacked, a son of his own."

"I could see where the lack of a son would cause great concern."

"He wasn't too concerned. In fact, I was to be his heir, but Elohim promised another. A son from my master's own loins would be his heir."

Her mouth fell open. "You were heir to Abraham's fortune?"

"That is a story for another time, but yes. Before Isaac, I was in line to inherit it all. When Abraham asked what Elohim had in mind, He told him to look up toward the night sky and count the stars." He waved upward, though there were no stars out in the late morning. "If Abraham were even able to count them, which of course he couldn't. Then He told him, so would his offspring be." Eliezer looked up at her. "And so, my dear, we carry the most precious cargo of all. You are to be Isaac's wife and the one who will bear those stars."

Rebekah's gaze went up to the clear sky. She imagined the blanket of darkness she had lain under countless times with its bright lights twinkling above her. On many nights, she too had attempted to count them and lost numbers before she ran out of stars. The feeling of her life being so insignificant in comparison to a god who held the exact count caught her breath. What plans did He hold for her?

Chapter 10

"Evening and morning and at noon I utter my
complaint and moan, and he hears my voice."
-Psalm 55:17

Beerlahairoi, 2025 B.C.
Isaac

Isaac adjusted the stake of his tent that had pulled up in the strong wind. After securing it in place, he walked in the field among his flock.

Jedidiah was about an arrow's shot away tending to the expanded group of animals. Tira, his beloved canine, and the other dogs patrolled the outer circle of livestock.

The fluffy sheep moved around Isaac as he passed. His thoughts were scattered and mingled. Ideas of his faraway bride invaded more and more with each passing day. Which dusty sky would herald her arrival?

He shook his head attempting to clear his mind, but the warring feelings of excitement and nervousness pulled at him. Would this woman he never met be a good match for him? Would she adjust to life in the fields?

"Elohim, I don't know if You'll listen to the son of Your servant, but the thing I thought would provide a step forward in my life is the thing I'm not sure will be a source of happiness. I don't know the name of my bride or even if Eliezer will be successful. I hope he was and at the same time, if everything stays as it is, I can live with that.

"Ishmael has produced great sons and daughters. He should be the one to inherit *Abba's* fortune and Your blessing." He looked up to the blazing sun. "I can't hear You. Are You even listening?"

The same silence that haunted him mocked him again. Not even a whisper of wind confirmed he had been heard.

He sighed and let his head and shoulders slouch. "If You do hear me, and if Eliezer was successful, protect my wife. Bring her to me safely. There are many dangers that lie in wait between here and her homeland. Guard her like I guard my flocks."

The bleating of sheep and rustling of animals grazing were the only sounds that returned his humble pleas.

Tira circled with two other dogs. Her full belly swung as she walked.

"Be her rearguard and her shield, Elohim." He watched the gentle giant sentinels. "Please. Even if You're not here with me."

Chapter 11

*"But Abram said, 'O Lord GOD, what will you give
me, for I continue childless, and the heir of my house
is Eliezer of Damascus?' "*
-Genesis 15:2

The King's Highway, 2025 B.C.
Rebekah

A glint of sunlight reflected off Eliezer's golden earring
into Rebekah's eyes. "I was admiring your earring."

He reached up, fingering the piece of metal. "My
mark."

"Mark?"

"Of service to my master." He looked up at her.
"You find the custom odd?"

"Actually, I used a similar technique to mark my
sheep. I carved my symbol into their ear to prove they
are...were mine."

"I was born into service." He twisted the gold loop,
then dropped his hand. "When Abraham came

through my town of Damascus, one of his wagons had sustained massive damage. My father was able to repair it. He chose to winter in the city. During his time there, he became close with my father and eventually purchased my father from his master."

"You've been with Abraham your whole life?"

"I've often thought of purchasing my freedom. My father eventually did."

"Why haven't you?"

He held up his chin. "I fell in love."

"With Abraham?"

He smiled and let out a deep chuckle. "With Elohim. And I guess, Abraham in a way. He is a very kind master and a good man."

She grew quiet for several moments. "And his son?"

"Is as good a master as any."

The praise made her smile.

"When I chose to stay, he took me to the post of his tent and used an awl to pierce my ear. Then he put this ring in the hole as a sign. This is a permanent mark of my willing servanthood and great love for my master. It also marked me as a lifetime member of his household."

"You enjoy being a servant?"

He thought for a moment. "Abraham is a different type of master."

She leaned closer. "Different how?"

"He confided in me early on that he heard from

Elohim. He spoke of his God as if it was the most natural thing in the world to hear from an invisible deity that no one else could hear. He even said…" His speech halted as if he were about to reveal a guarded secret.

"Said what?"

"I told you before that he wanted to name me his heir. He said he had even made the suggestion to Elohim."

"What happened?"

"Elohim had other plans. Abraham told me Elohim had promised him a son, even in his advanced age. That son would be Abraham's heir. Not me."

"Isaac?"

He nodded with a slight grin. "Isaac."

"Do you ever feel that Isaac stole your blessing?"

"Oh my, no. What right does a servant have to usurp a son?" He shook his head and waved his free hand. "If Abraham had given me all he had, then I would certainly be blessed. But that's just it. It would have only blessed me. Through Isaac, through you, Elohim has promised to bless the world. That is far better."

Rebekah's gaze returned to the horizon as her next words tumbled out low, "Have you ever heard from Elohim?"

"Not directly." He hesitated. "Master Abraham has taught me to listen, but I don't hear a voice as he does. I did see the visitors, but they did not speak to me.

Elohim chooses to speak in different ways."

"I just keep thinking, how can one worship a god they can't see?"

He chewed on his inner cheek. "It's hard to describe, but just because something can't be seen doesn't mean it doesn't exist and in great force, mind you. Take, for example, the wind."

"The wind?"

"As one who walks the fields, you know of such, yes?"

She rolled her eyes. "Of course."

"How? It can't be seen with your eyes."

As if by command, a breeze kicked up and blew her hair about her face.

"You know the wind exists because you've felt and experienced it for yourself, such is Elohim. Just as the wind blows strong enough to move sand dunes as large as mountains, such is Elohim. Just as powerful as the wind can blow so that the strongest man or beast cannot stand against it, such is Elohim."

She straightened as she thought on his words.

"And what of love?" he continued.

"Love?"

"It too can't be seen with the eyes, yet you have felt and experienced it, yes?"

Rebekah thought of her father's comfortable embrace and the rare but proud smile of her mother. "Yes."

"Love can wrap you up so tight that its warmth

reaches so deep inside you pray it never leaves. It can soften a heart of stone and turn back a wayward child. Such is Elohim."

She sighed a shallow sigh thinking of a god with the strength of the wind and the embrace of love.

"You know your family didn't always worship strange gods." He turned the camels' reins to adjust their course. "There was a time your people followed Elohim. You remember Adam and Eve?"

She smiled and nodded.

"Their children had children who had children. The lessons from Elohim were passed from parent to child. Enoch walked with Elohim until he was no more. Noah too heard the voice of Elohim and obeyed. Somewhere along the way, people stopped listening to him until Abraham listened."

"So why doesn't my family?"

"It is just as those who seek out concubines. They fear missing out or perhaps listen more to their fleshly desires. So, your family too traded their relationship with Elohim for others who falsely promised security. They allowed their hearts to be led astray. Elohim loves them so much that He gave them over to their desires in hopes that one day, when their true needs remained unmet, they would return to their first love. Sadly, they haven't."

Had she ever felt love from a deity? Fear and favor, yes, but love? Could she love a man who was a stranger to her? Could she love Elohim who was just as strange to her? Could a strange god love her?

His strong voice rang out through the empty ravine they pressed through, "I knew Elohim heard me the day we met."

"How?"

"I was praying and asking Him to show me the exact woman He wanted for Isaac. I asked Him to reveal to me a woman who would show compassion to me as well as my camels without me asking." He navigated over the rocks and around the boulders. "Before I was even done talking, I saw you come down the path. You filled your water jug and came up out of the well. I remember thinking how beautiful you were and how much my master would be pleased with a choice like you."

Rebekah felt heat rise in her cheeks. She had barely taken notice of the old man, yet she had been the answer to his prayers.

"Of course, I had to make sure the inside matched the outside." He flicked a playful look over his shoulder. "When practically the same words I had used to ask Elohim for a sign fell from your lips, I knew you were the one He had chosen."

Her gaze bounced around the sides of the stony walls. She still wasn't sure she was the right choice.

A loud bark and ear-piercing scream from behind caught Rebekah's attention. She nearly toppled from the top of her camel as she twisted to see behind her. Hadiya was on the next camel and was also turned around straining to see what had caused the commotion. Deborah rode on the third camel; her hands covered her mouth and her eyes were set on a high cliff and were wide with panic. Zami was in a defense position barking at the cliffs in a frenzy.

"Deborah," Rebekah called out. "What did you see?"

Before the nurse could speak, men poured from the cliffs above like a fast-flowing river. Each lifted a curved blade and held hunger in their eyes.

Rebekah turned to find Eliezer still holding the lead camel's reins. His grip tightened for a moment before he released the leather. "Stay up there," he ordered and rushed toward the back of the caravan.

Layth pulled a curved blade from his belt and charged the nearest man.

The camel under Rebekah froze. She felt his thick muscles tense. Her own body reacted in kind. She was helpless sitting atop the beast, but would be in even greater danger if she attempted to dismount.

Eliezer tried to push the far camels closer into a circle, but the frightened animals appeared stuck in the sands.

Taj, Dov, and Meir joined Layth in defending the caravan.

Zami took off into the group, and Rebekah lost sight of him.

Rebekah caught Deborah's still frozen panicked expression. She lifted a hand in some effort to comfort her. It was a feeble attempt as there was nothing she could do.

The four guards pushed toward the sea of bandits trying to keep them from the three women. Like a wall of water breaking free, the thieves poured over the men with lifted swords.

They headed straight for the camels loaded with supplies and possessions. With filthy hands, they grabbed at sacks and pulled ties free. Camels bucked and hissed at the men. One man raised his sword to the throat of a defiant camel and, with one clean slice, the animal dropped to the ground.

Rebekah lifted a hand to her pulsing throat. Would hers be next?

Another bandit rushed toward Deborah who sat motionless, never blinking. Hadiya swiftly kicked at one who came near her camel. The men fought to pull the two women from their seats.

Rebekah willed her arms to move and yanked her camel's reins to turn him around. The beast unwillingly obeyed and turned. She pressed her camel between Hadiya and the man who tried to pull her down, pushing him aside with the weight of the creature.

The man's dark eyes brightened as if he had gained a far better prize.

"Rebekah, no!" Hadiya's voice lifted to a shrill behind her.

She turned to see her handmaid attempt to order

her camel to sit. When the beast did not move, Hadiya awkwardly toppled into the sand.

Rebekah pushed her camel harder, attempting to press the man further away from her nurse and handmaid. "Run, Hadiya!"

The woman disobeyed and went charging toward the man.

Rebekah hopped off her camel, landing hard. Thankfully, the soft sand gave under her to brace her fall. She rose before she had properly gotten her bearings and tumbled forward into the sand. Scrambling to get her feet under her, she charged after Hadiya.

The handmaid reached the man first and threw her weight into him. She might as well have been a feather trying to knock down a fortified city for as much impact as she had on the burly man.

With reflexes as fast as a lightning strike, the man caught Hadiya's arm and lifted her off her feet. He held her up to his body and moved to wrap his arm around her midsection.

Rebekah stopped short of the bandit and tried to make herself appear as large as possible. "Unhand my maid."

The man's greasy smile met her demand. He lifted his curved blade at her. "Don't worry. You're both in good hands."

Rebekah's grip felt empty without her shepherd's rod. If she had only kept her tools, she would be able to teach this beast of a man a lesson.

Sounds of clanging metal and manly grunts surrounded them. Zami's continued barks rang out around them as they bounced off the high stone walls.

The memories of the leopard, wolf, and all the other desert creatures she had defeated to protect her precious sheep came flooding back to her. She had been prepared to handle them. She had been brave and strong. Now, looking at Hadiya's desperate and pained expression, Rebekah was without resources and powerless to help. Why had Abraham's god brought her on this journey just to end up in the hands of bandits?

Fear and courage mingled their way through her blood. Her cheeks flamed hot as her heart and breath quickened. "Release my handmaid this instant."

He chuckled and tightened his grip on Hadiya's arm. "Or what, desert flower?" He flicked his head behind him. "The others have your guards well taken care of. Soon all this will be mine." His smile widened. "In fact,…" He tossed Hadiya.

Rebekah watched her handmaid's body hit a nearby pile of rocks hard and then unnaturally roll to the ground. She gasped and went running toward her.

The man reached out and snatched Rebekah before she could get far. "I think I'll just take my reward." His tight grip on her arm was flaming hot and coiled like a snake as he dragged her closer. "Right now."

The stench of his breath scorched her face as he breathed on her. The odor of men living in the caves of the wilderness was pungent and sent Rebekah's stomach flipping.

He pulled her closer and tighter to himself.

She dug at his grip, tearing at his flesh, but couldn't find release.

The thoughts of Hadiya and Deborah being handled by these men cut deep into Rebekah. They had willingly followed her to their demise. Thoughts of home, of her mother and brother, of all her uncles, aunts, and cousins rushed over her like a sorrow-filled wave. Tears blinded her and blurred the man's face. Sobs threatened at her lips as she bit them back.

A large figure moved in her side vision, and she blinked away her tears just in time to see Zami leap toward the man.

The man's scream rang in Rebekah's ears as he released his grip on her, causing her to stumble and fall to the ground.

Light reflected off his curved blade as she watched him plunge it into Zami's side.

"No!" She reached out to her dog.

As the two tussled in the sand, Rebekah saw that Zami's bite had landed securely around the bandit's throat. He plunged long teeth deeper into the flesh as blood seeped from the penetrations. The massive canine thrashed back and forth causing the wounds to tear open. Thick crimson blood splattered onto Zami, speckling his golden coat.

The bandit pressed his blade further while his free hand tore at Zami's golden fur. He was successful in pulling out chunks of hair, but Zami did not relent.

Rebekah moved to Hadiya as she kept an eye on the two locked in combat. She put a trembling hand to Hadiya's nose and open mouth. A slight breath came out, but just barely enough to be felt. She moved to place herself between the woman and the fight.

A horrific gurgling sound came from the bandit as Zami tightened his hold on the man's throat.

Giving up his grip on his sword and Zami's fur, the bandit reached for the dog's jaws in an attempt to pry them open.

Zami growled and tightened his grasp.

The man dug his heels into the sand, pressing up and back attempting to separate himself from the lethal hold.

The dog planted his feet on the man's shoulders, pressing him further into the sand. With a violent rip, Zami removed a large chunk of the bandit's neck sealing the scoundrel's fate.

"Zami," Rebekah whispered.

The dog stood over the lifeless remains, hesitating. She tried again, "Zami."

His ear turned backward toward her, but his gaze remained fixed on the potential threat in front of him.

She whistled low.

With backward steps, the dog finally relented and

came toward her. Blood poured from the wound in his side. The handle of the blade hung low, almost dragging in the sand. In his mouth hung a hunk of flesh and muscle.

With quivering fingers, Rebekah reached for the handle of the sword.

"Don't!" Eliezer grabbed her hand.

She looked up into his bloody and beaten face.

"Wait till I find something to put pressure on the wound before you touch that blade." He hurried away to rummage through the scattered belongings and managed to find a few strips of cloth. "This might do." He handed her the material. "I'll pull out the blade, you get that bandage on as fast as possible."

She took the linen in her hands.

He put a hand on the blade's handle. "Ready?"

She nodded.

"Now!" He pulled hard.

Blood poured from the wound as Rebekah tied the material as quickly and tightly as she could.

Zami yelped.

"You're going to be alright, boy." She tied a double knot and ran her fingers over his head. "You're going to be alright." Her gaze lifted to the scene around her.

Taj knelt on the other side of Hadiya. His clothes were torn, and his face held similar beatings to Eliezer's. With a gentle hand on Hadiya's neck, he felt for a pulse.

The memory of her hitting the rocks made

Rebekah's stomach flip. "Is she…"

"She's still breathing. I think she just took a hard blow to the head."

Eliezer waved to Dov. "Round up what you can. We must get out of here as quickly as possible. I don't know if they plan on returning."

He nodded and circled the remaining camels.

The other men helped by picking up what bags and supplies they could find and securing them to the animals.

Rebekah looked around. None of the bandits were in sight save the one Zami had taken care of. "What happened?"

"A conversation for a safer place." Eliezer kept an eye on his surroundings. "We need to get out of here."

"Where to?"

"Damascus. It's close."

Dov helped Deborah onto her camel while Taj lifted Hadiya's body into her waiting arms. The older woman instinctively tucked the young girl into her embrace as the camel rose to his feet.

Meir reached out his hand to Rebekah. "Mistress."

She placed her hand in his and rose to her shaking feet.

He held onto her as they walked to the waiting camel and he helped her mount her ride. Then he returned to scoop Zami into his arms.

Rebekah held out her hands. "I'll take him."

"You're sure?" He adjusted Zami's body. "This

beast is heavy."

"I'm sure." She motioned for him to come close.

Meir hoisted the dog onto Rebekah's lap and then ordered the camel to rise.

Zami let out a faint whimper with the movement.

Rebekah held tight to him. "How far are we from the city?"

"Not far." Eliezer scanned the horizon. "We should make it before nightfall."

As the thinned group traveled the few hours to Damascus, Rebekah kept her eyes on the red stain that grew larger on the bandaged side of her dog. Flashes of panther teeth, swords, and blood vied for her attention. She had faced this battle before and came out victorious. She glanced back to the camel behind her carrying Deborah and Hadiya. Their faces and arms held scratches and scrapes, but at least they were alive. Her gaze fell back to the companion on her lap. His breath became more labored with every moment that passed.

She intertwined her fingers in his golden fur as she whispered to him as she used to in the wilderness before she agreed to leave everything behind and go on this foolish journey. Tears clung to her lashes. How could they be ambushed? Wasn't Abraham's god protecting them?

Chapter 12

"But Abram said, 'O Lord GOD, what will you give me, for I continue childless, and the heir of my house is Eliezer of Damascus?' "
-Genesis 15:2

Damascus, 2025 B.C.
Rebekah

The fading light of day retreated as Rebekah's caravan came over the last crest toward their destination. Damascus sat like a jewel on a brown pillow as they limped into the city.

Eliezer pushed the group deeper until they came upon a long row of buildings. At one, he stopped and pounded on the door.

With a creak, the door opened far enough for Rebekah to see a young servant girl fill the small void.

"May I help you?" The woman's eyes flicked to each member of the group.

"I'm Eliezer. Would you please fetch the Master of the house?"

She nodded and shut the door.

Only a heartbeat passed for Rebekah before the door flew open again. An older couple appeared at the threshold tugging Eliezer inside. The man was bent slightly with age, but his clasp on Eliezer was strong. Next to him was a woman whose gray hair stuck out from under a beautiful, deep blue headwrap.

"My son has been returned!" the woman screamed. She gripped Eliezer as if he would float away if she let him go.

The older man beamed with pride. "It's good to see you, my son." His eyes were the same deep, dark, and childlike orbs of Eliezer's. Their hereditary link was undeniable.

"It's good to be seen, Father." Eliezer tried to take a step back, but his parents' hold on him would not be surrendered. "But I'm afraid my arrival is not one of good fortune. We have wounds that must be tended."

Eliezer's mother held him out to arm's length. "Wounds? Where?" Light from an oil lamp behind them lit Eliezer's face as she inspected him. Scrapes bled and the coloring of bruises started to come to the surface. "What happened?"

He held her wrists gently. "I will explain all once we've been treated."

It was only then that the couple peered around their son to see the rest of the group.

Eliezer's mother held her hands to her open mouth. "Oh. Please, come in at once." She lifted the hem of her dress and waved them inside. Rebekah watched her form disappear, but heard her call, "Renna, get some fresh water and clean linens."

Taj came near Rebekah, ordered her camel to lay, and lifted his arms.

Rebekah gently shifted Zami into his waiting arms. Her wrist burned with the movement, but she ignored the pain. She dismounted her camel swiftly and followed closely behind him.

When she entered the large house, the immediate sense of warmth engulfed her. The bottom floor was divided with a large open area to one side and a mirrored area on the other which was separated into stalls laid with fresh straw.

Eliezer brought in the remaining four camels to inspect them.

"Over here." Eliezer's mother motioned Taj to an open area. "You can set him there."

The young servant girl had set out bowls of clean water and stacked fresh linens. She brought in a tray of assorted bottles and containers.

Taj carefully set Zami down at the older woman's feet.

Rebekah caught her dog wince as she knelt beside him.

Eliezer's father went to lift the bandage.

Zami growled.

"Better let me." Rebekah moved closer. "He's not fond of strangers."

He eased back.

She gently untied the wrapped bandage. Blood leaked from the large, open wound.

The man's brow furrowed. "I don't like the look of that." He pressed on the dog's side.

Zami yelped and pawed at the ground trying to get away.

"Easy, boy." Rebekah reached over and rubbed his head. "They are here to help you."

The dog relaxed under her touch.

Eliezer's father grabbed a cloth and set to work cleaning the wound. "I assume he belongs to you?"

"More like I belong to his flock." Hot tears stung her eyes. "He was just trying to protect me."

"It seems you all have quite a story to tell."

She followed his eyes to the group of bloody and beaten men, women, and camels surrounding them in the space. Then she glanced back. "We are grateful for your help."

He closed his eyes and nodded. "Excuse me." With a hand on his knee, he braced himself to stand and then made his way to Eliezer.

Rebekah watched as the two men spoke in hushed tones. Eliezer's father twisted the dirty cloth in his hands as his words became more forced. She intertwined her fingers in Zami's thick fur and counted more heartbeats between his breaths.

Eliezer stepped closer to his father, his eyes and hands pleading.

His father looked to the packed earth and shook his head.

Eliezer stepped around him and came to kneel beside Rebekah. His watery eyes told her all she needed to know. "My father thinks—"

"I know." She kept her eyes focused on the distance. "Nothing can be done."

A warm hand covered hers. "I'm sorry. The damage…it's too great."

She allowed tears to spill over without attempting to hold them back.

"We can make him comfortable, but I'm afraid…"

She closed her eyes and nodded as she bit on her bottom lip until she tasted blood. More hot tears slid down her cheeks.

"I'm so sorry."

"Me too." She pulled Zami's large head onto her lap and pressed her forehead onto his. "I'm sorry, boy."

Eliezer rose and returned to his inspection of the camels.

The others withdrew too, seeming to give Rebekah much needed space.

She hummed her favorite tune in Zami's ear and ached for her flute to play for him one last time.

Zami closed his golden eyes and relaxed deeply into her embrace.

When her throat became too parched to hum, she rocked him gently to the melody.

After a few quiet moments, Zami let out a short

breath and didn't take in another.

Rebekah stroked his long back and simply allowed his comforting presence to envelop her once more. "I don't know what I'm going to do without you, Zami." She buried her face into his coat and wept until no more tears could be summoned.

She felt a strong hand on her shoulder and looked up.

Eliezer's father stood behind her with tear streaks on his cheeks. "I'll take care of him. Why don't you let my wife tend to your injuries?"

She looked down at her dog. "I don't think I can let him go."

"You don't have to." He knelt and patted the dog's head. "He is always going to be with you. Guarding you wherever you go."

A short smile creased her lips. "You think so?"

"I know so. Why, a dog as loyal as this one couldn't do anything but stay with you."

She nodded and hugged Zami tight. "I didn't say it often enough, but thank you, boy."

As she relaxed her grip, Taj lifted the dog into his arms. "It would be my honor to help."

Taj and Eliezer's father took Zami out of the house through the back door.

Eliezer's mother came to stand next to Rebekah. "Are you hurt, my dear?"

"I'm not really sure." She rubbed her wrist. "My arm burns a little."

The older woman held out her hands, palms up, and wiggled her fingers. "Better let me have a look."

She consented to the examination.

With delicate movements, the woman worked her way up and down Rebekah's hand and arm. "Maybe a little sprain, but I don't think anything is broken. We should wrap it just in case." She snatched a clean cloth and had Rebekah's wrist tied securely before she could argue.

"Where did you learn how to take care of injuries?"

She smiled. "I was a midwife for a very long time. Though my hands aren't strong enough to catch babies anymore," she tapped the side of her head, "nothing can take away my knowledge."

She pulled in her arm and hugged it to her body. "Thank you for your kindness."

"No thanks needed. We would do anything for our boy." She glanced at Eliezer who stood among the camels.

"Your son is a very wise man."

"Experience is a grand teacher."

Rebekah tilted her head.

She reached for another cloth and dipped it in the water before reaching out to Rebekah. "Let's clean up these other cuts on you. Infections can be nasty things."

No one had to tell her such a truth. Her thoughts went immediately to her father. An infection had stolen him away, and now the sword of a bandit had cut out the other being closest to her heart.

The cool water felt nice on her skin as she sat still under the care of the old midwife. Though her heart ached with sorrow and she was completely drained, the warmth of the woman and her home drew her in. "I'm sorry, but in the rush to seek treatment, I don't believe I caught your name."

"Zahar and my husband is Ori." She gently wiped Rebekah's face and hands.

"I'm called Rebekah." She flinched at the sting of the ointments. "And Eliezer is your son?"

She nodded; clear pride beaming from her eyes.

"Do you have any other children?"

Darkness washed over her face and she took a long breath before answering. "No others. I've been barren all my life."

She pulled back. "I thought you said Eliezer was your son?"

"The son of my heart, but not of my womb." She rinsed off the cloth in the bowl. "We adopted him."

"I see."

Their servant, Renna, came down the ladder. "The meal is set."

Zahar held out a hand. "Come, my dear. Let's get some food into you, and then I will show you where you can rest."

Rebekah extended her uninjured hand and stood to her feet. She followed Zahar up the ladder to the second floor. A long table was covered in dishes varying in offerings. Soft pillows lined the two sides for reclining.

The others followed them up and stood around the room.

Ori waved toward the table. "Please, sit wherever you'd like."

They settled around the table in silence. The air was heavy with loss and pain.

Rebekah reclined on a lovely crimson pillow as she waited for their host.

Ori lounged at the head of the table and bowed in a short, but heartfelt prayer. When he finished, he motioned for them to eat.

The men wasted no time in diving into the bounty. Deborah and Hadiya were not as eager, but ate with modesty.

Rebekah sat staring at the bowls and platters. She knew she needed to fill her empty stomach, but her hollow heart kept her from reaching out.

Zahar sat a bowl full of stew and a hunk of bread in front of her. "You need your strength."

The scent of warm spices filled Rebekah's nose. Her stomach urged her to partake.

Zahar patted her hand. "Just try."

Rebekah nodded and pulled a small piece of bread. She dipped it into the waiting stew and popped the portion into her mouth. A rush of deep flavors filled her from the inside. Nothing had ever tasted so good. With wide eyes, she turned toward her hostess.

Zahar smiled. "Family recipe."

"You must teach me."

She nodded. "I'd be happy to."

After the group had emptied the platters, Renna cleared them and returned with more, filled with cheese and fresh fruit. She placed one in the center stacked with a special treat.

Zahar took one of the ringed pieces of bread and set it in front of Rebekah. "It's called *ka'ak*."

She lifted the small circle to her mouth and savored a bite.

"Another family recipe."

"It's delicious."

The others took pieces and emptied the rest of the platters in record time.

"Now, son," Ori began. "Are you going to tell us what happened to you?"

Eliezer's gaze flicked to Rebekah and then the men before answering, "I was sent to Padanaram to fetch a bride for my master's son. We were escorting Rebekah back to my master when we were ambushed." A tangle of emotions choked his words. "We made it out alive, but not without paying a price." He looked up to meet the soft gaze of his father. "Several of my master's camels were killed in the attack. Thankfully it seems we got away with only minor injuries, though many of our supplies and my master's possessions were taken."

Rebekah looked around to see the men and her two female companions freshly bandaged, though no one looked seriously damaged.

Tears swam in Eliezer's bright eyes. "I've failed my master."

Ori eased back on his stack of pillows. "Was your task to bring back the same number of camels and possessions?"

Eliezer furrowed his brow. "My duty was to find a wife for Abraham's son."

The older man's tender gaze fell on Rebekah. "And I see you have succeeded in doing so."

"I did."

"Then it seems you have not failed your master at all."

"I suppose you're right." Eliezer wiped his face with the back of his sleeve. "But we still have a long way to travel before my task is complete."

"But first, you will rest and heal. When you are ready, we will make sure you have what you need."

"Thank you, Father."

Rebekah's eyes grew heavy, and she swayed.

"Come, child," Zahar's voice was soft in her ear. "I'll show you where you and your women can sleep."

The woman guided them up to the third floor and into a room with stacks of blankets and pillows.

"Rest. I shall see you in the morning."

Hadiya laid a few blankets out and took Rebekah to the pile. "Sleep well, Mistress."

Rebekah had her doubts, but as soon as her head hit the pile of pillows she slipped effortlessly into sleep.

Chapter 13

"And Isaac came from the way of the well Lahairoi;
for he dwelt in the south country."
-Genesis 24:62

Beerlahairoi, 2025 B.C.
Isaac

Isaac rubbed the side of his panting dog, Tira. "Not much longer, girl."

The dog's breathing quickened with her labor. She whimpered through the pain.

"Nice and easy." He stroked her fur. "We've done this before. Keep breathing."

Jedidiah stood behind him. "How much longer do you think?"

"She's pretty close."

"I'll get some water."

Isaac's eyes darted to the back end of Tira waiting for signs of the first birth.

Jedidiah returned with a bowl of clean water and

set it near Tira's head. "Drink up, girl. You'll need your strength."

The dog lapped a few sips and then laid her head down again.

Isaac watched her tense and start to quiver. "I think it's time." He adjusted to get a better viewpoint.

Jedidiah knelt beside Tira's head. "Push, girl."

The dog bore down as liquid trickled from her back end. She turned around to lick at it. Then she got up to adjust her position.

Moments later, her tail lifted as a clear sack slowly emerged. After several more pushes, the sack gently slid out.

Tira reached around to lick and bite at the sack until it burst open revealing a fawn-colored puppy. She roughly licked at it until they all heard a tiny yelp.

A smile played at Isaac's mouth.

"Male or female?"

Isaac gently lifted the puppy's hind leg as Tira chewed on the cord. "Male."

"Got names chosen?"

Isaac cut his eyes at his friend.

"Of course, you do." He shook his head. "Out with it."

Isaac rubbed the small tan fluff. "Habi."

Jedidiah chuckled.

Tira cleaned her first pup and nudged him toward her waiting teat.

Shadows descended on the fields as Tira welcomed her sixth puppy.

"Another male." Isaac lifted the last puppy and placed him next to Tira's bloated belly.

Jedidiah rubbed Tira's head. "Well done, girl. That makes four, and two females."

Isaac eased back to sit next to his dog.

His companion slapped him on the back. "Congratulations. They all seem very healthy."

"Tira did a great job. She is so motherly; I didn't expect anything less from her."

"So, let me see if I can remember everyone." Jedidiah touched the first one and moved down the row of suckling puppies. "Habi, Adena, Hadar, Asa, Hava, and…"

"Amit."

"Amit." He stroked the last boy. "They certainly are a good-looking group."

"I can't wait to see them with the flocks and get a feel for their abilities."

"If they are anything like their parents, you are going to have a tough time keeping them away from their duty."

"I see congratulations are in order," a voice boomed behind them.

Isaac turned to look up into the face of his brother. "Ishmael." He rose to embrace him. "What are you doing in Beerlahairoi?"

"I had some business out this way and figured I'd visit you for a change."

"The honor is mine."

Ishmael glanced around his brother to the suckling litter. "Isn't new life glorious?"

Isaac beamed at his new pack and nodded.

"Wait till you hold your own child. It's even better."

A flutter of despair flickered in Isaac's gut. Was that something waiting for him?

Jedidiah perked up. "Isaac's bride is on her way."

Ishmael caught his brother's glance. "Truly?"

"My father sent a servant to his homeland in search of one. I'm not sure when they will return. It's a very long journey."

"From Ur?"

"Padanaram; where our distant family still lives."

"I see." He rubbed his chin. "Well, when she does arrive, you'll have to make sure to bring her to Kadesh so I can have the pleasure of meeting her."

"Of course."

Ishmael's gaze traveled back to the feasting brood. "How old are they?"

"Mere hours."

"Hours?" His eyes widened. "They're massive."

"All very healthy and normal size for their breed."

"I can see why they are popular among you shepherds. If I were a hungry predator, I'd think twice before trying to capture anything guarded by a group of those."

"That's the idea."

"I must have one for my home."

Isaac held his mouth open to answer, but Jedidiah interjected, "They don't really do well as indoor dogs. They're more bred for work outside."

Ishmael wrinkled his forehead at his brother. "What does he mean?"

"I specifically breed these dogs to live with the sheep and be on guard outside. They thrive on doing that duty. If you were to try to bring them inside for simple companionship," he hesitated, "I just don't think they would behave well."

"What if I used the dog more as an outside guard? It could live in the courtyard and keep watch."

Isaac thought about the idea for several moments. "I'm not really sure. I've never bred them for that type of labor. It sounds like it could work, but I couldn't guarantee the dog would do what you want. Everyone who comes onto your property would be seen as a threat unless you brought them there."

"So, I wouldn't have uninvited guests." His eyebrows danced. "That is entirely the point."

Isaac hung his head. "They won't be weaned from their mother for several weeks. Why don't I think about it and try my hand at some different training? When the time comes, at least I can say I gave it my best effort."

Ishmael reached out his hand and placed it on his brother's shoulder. "That's all I can ask."

Isaac looked up into his brother's face expecting to see harshness or at least disappointment, but all he saw was understanding. "I can promise I'll try, but I can't promise it will work. If I feel the dog would not thrive in the situation, will you give me your word not to press the matter further?"

He squeezed his shoulder. "Of course, of course. Now," he clapped his hands and rubbed them together, "do I get to choose?"

"It seems fair. Though with them being only hours old, I don't really know their personalities. As the days go by, I might have a better chance of success if I observe their natural behaviors first. I wouldn't want to give you a dog that is completely wrong for your wishes."

"That's a fair point." He crossed his arms over his chest. "Then I shall leave the choice with you."

"Thank you, brother."

Ishmael smiled. "I do like hearing that." The smile shifted. "Well, I must return to my business."

"You can't stay for a meal?"

He waved his hands in front of himself. "No, no. I truly must be going. Though I shall return in a few months to meet my new guard." He gave a quick wink then took his leave.

As Isaac watched his brother's form disappear, he met glances with Jedidiah.

The other shepherd stood there staring him down. "What?"

"I can't believe you just agreed to that madness. Our dogs aren't house dogs. They are bred as tools to do our job. Our livelihood depends on them and now you're just handing them out to sit at Ishmael's feet?"

"You heard him; he wants one for a guard. It's not that far a leap from sheep guard to human guard."

"You've never tried it before."

"I've never had anyone request it before."

Jedidiah shook his head. "Perfect waste of a good dog if you ask me."

"I didn't ask you. Remember your place, Jedidiah."

"Oh, I remember my place." His eyes burned hot. "Do you know yours?" Without waiting for an answer, he turned and headed toward the flock.

Isaac knelt beside Tira and gave her head a gentle rub. "The problem is, he's right." He smoothed her coat and used his finger to stroke each puppy. "I thought I knew my place, but why am I here in Beerlahairoi as my mother's body rots in a cave in Machpelah, and my father has his mat warmed by a woman young enough to be my older sister?"

He picked up one of the puppies and tucked her close to him. "What does Elohim truly have planned for me?"

Chapter 14

"Now the LORD said to Abram, 'Go from your country and your kindred and your father's house to the land that I will show you.' "
-Genesis 12:1

Damascus, 2025 B.C.
Rebekah

Rebekah watched the simmering stew over the open flame. Warm scents filled her nose and spread through her entire body. She let out a deep sigh.

Eliezer's mother, Zahar, watched her from across the room. "Good cooking makes you feel good from the inside out, doesn't it?"

Rebekah dipped her little finger into the stew and lifted it to her mouth for a taste. "I always knew food was important. I just never realized it could be this good."

"Your mother never taught you?" She sliced through a fresh cucumber.

"She taught me what she could." She shrugged and returned to stirring. "When I was home anyway."

Zahar's hand held the end of the blade still. "When you were home? Where else would you be?"

"I was actually a shepherdess. I only spent about half the year home and the other in the wilderness of Padanaram."

"Oh my. That sounds very dangerous."

"It was more my home than the place my family dwelt." She lifted her fingers to trace the fading scabs on her cheek. "Safer than some places I've been."

Zahar set her knife down and used a rag to wipe off her hands as she made her way over to Rebekah. She placed a gentle palm on Rebekah's other cheek. "Our enemies never fight fair."

"That may be true," Eliezer stepped into the kitchen, "but Elohim promises to be with us in the dangers. In this, He shows His strength in our weakness. He shows His might in our hopelessness. He shows His power in our powerlessness. He shows He is God, and we are not."

Zahar beamed.

Rebekah turned away to return her focus to the stew.

Zahar patted her hand and left the two alone.

Eliezer stood near Rebekah. "You've been quiet the past couple of days."

"I've been doing a lot of thinking."

"And what has this time of pondering wrought?"

"I have a question about your master."

"Speak on."

"Why did Abram choose to change his name to Abraham?"

"He didn't."

She lifted a thin brow at him.

"Elohim gave him a new name. That is a very interesting story. Would you like to hear it?"

She nodded.

"It was actually Abraham's father Terah who had the idea to leave Ur. He heard Haran was becoming a grand city. So, one day, they packed all their goods into a few four-wheeled carts drawn by oxen and headed to Haran.

"When they made it there, Terah found favor among the bustling city and settled on its outskirts. He and Abraham were idol makers, working with wood and metal to create beautiful carvings for people to worship."

Rebekah thought back to her family's Inanna statues. She knew they had been carved by her Great Grandfather's hand and held a special place in her father's heart.

"Even in his deepest devotion, my master found it difficult to truly worship something that had been carved by man's hand." Eliezer allowed his chin to drop to his chest. "When he started following Elohim, he realized he'd much rather devote his life to a God who made him with His hand.

"One day, Abraham heard the voice of Elohim calling for him to leave Haran. When he told his father Terah, you can imagine the pain and disappointment he experienced. His own son, the one who would follow his path of being an idol maker, wanted to follow a god that didn't require the creation of an idol. No idol meant no profit. No profit meant no food in the family's stomachs.

"Abraham was insistent that they leave Haran and follow the call. Terah wasn't convinced. He didn't hear the call and neither did the rest of the family.

"But Elohim was calling Abraham to leave. Out of respect for his patriarch, Abraham stayed put until his father's death released him to obey the call of Elohim."

He looked up at her. "His caravan included his wife Sarah, his nephew Lot, and all the servants and livestock that belonged to him. They traveled in the direction Elohim revealed."

Rebekah chewed on her lips for a few moments as she stirred the stew. "Why do you follow Elohim?"

"If I hadn't met Abraham and been introduced to Elohim, my life would have been…" His eyes misted. "Well, what all lives do when separated from our life source, wither and die."

"I don't see how Elohim is so very different from the gods of my people."

"Your gods and goddesses sit in their grand temples demanding service. Elohim reached down into the mud and got His hands dirty to create life. He continues even today to reach down into the dirt of our lives to help us stand. In your culture, you get to choose the gods you serve. Elohim chooses whoever He wants to use. He chooses us." Eliezer pointed to himself, then his finger moved to her. "He chooses you."

She rubbed absentmindedly at her bandaged wrist. "Why would he choose me?"

"He is allowed to extend a covenantal offering of love to anyone. Especially to those seemingly the most unworthy."

"I certainly feel unworthy."

"I did as well." He smirked. "I never was arrogant enough to believe the gods of my homeland would listen to a servant who had nothing to offer them. But Abraham explained it differently.

"The covenant that was extended to him included a special confirmation; a name change. By changing his name, Elohim was in a sense changing his destiny. No longer was he simply a 'father', but a 'father of a multitude'.

"He told me Elohim would ask me to bring myself first, as was requested of him. Then I could make an acceptable offering."

"And so, you did?"

"I surrendered myself to Him, then Abraham taught me to bring a worthy offering."

"So, you follow Abraham's god because you believed Abraham?"

"I follow Elohim because I heard the call."

Rebekah's eyes widened. "You did?"

He nodded slowly.

"How?"

"A voice I didn't recognize. A voice I don't even know if I really heard." He chuckled.

"More like a whisper you don't hear with your ears."

"Exactly like that." He tilted his head at her. "How do you know?"

She tucked her head. "I hear a voice call me, but I don't recognize it either. It's like a stranger."

"If you learn to listen to Him, His voice will become more familiar. It is Elohim that calls you, Rebekah."

"But I don't belong to his fold. How can a sheep learn to hear a stranger's voice?"

"Only when that stranger truly becomes the sheep's shepherd will the sheep learn." He pulled at his long, gray beard. "You left your sheep in your brother's care, correct?"

She nodded.

"In time, they will learn to trust his voice as their shepherd. You are not the first to hear the call of The Stranger. When your great uncle heard Him, he followed. But it's a choice. You must choose for yourself."

Zahar stepped back into the kitchen. "I do love having all these strong bodies around. Those men of yours have fixed every squeaky board in this house and cleaned our courtyard. I think I'll have to keep you all here forever."

Rebekah looked up into Eliezer's eyes.

A mix of joy and sadness washed over him before he turned to face his mother. "I wish we could, Mother, and you've been kind enough to provide us a safe harbor while we healed. A week is more than enough time. We'll be leaving at first light."

Zahar looked past him to Rebekah. "I understand. It would be wrong of me to stand in the path Elohim has for this young one." She smiled a warm smile that gripped Rebekah's heart. "We shall feast tonight and fill your camels with supplies." She crossed the room and took Rebekah's hands in her own. "I wish you a safe journey and all the blessings a woman's life can hold."

Rebekah wrapped her arms around the woman and held on to her. For the first time on the long journey, she missed her own mother. She tightened her embrace as Zahar hugged her back. "Thank you for your kindness. May it be repaid back to you a hundred-fold over."

As the last moments of night released their grasp on the breaking day, Rebekah stood in the doorway of Eliezer's parents' home. She clung tight to Zahar wishing beyond all hope she could simply stay put in this place of warmth and safety.

The sound of men packing camels behind her grated in her ears. They may as well have been playing flutes out of tune trying to tempt her away.

Tears burned as the blur of oil lamp light flooded Rebekah's vision. "I'm not sure I want to go."

"You must," Zahar whispered against her hair. "Your bridegroom is waiting for you."

"I can't thank you enough for all you've done for us. For me."

The older woman moved her hands to cup Rebekah's face. She wiped away a few stray tears and held her gaze. "I will be praying for you, sweet child."

Rebekah could see her dark eyes fill with tears.

"If Elohim ever brings your path back this way, make sure you stop in."

Her throat tightened to the point she could only nod.

Zahar pulled her in for another extended embrace.

Rebekah held on for as long as she could.

Ori came up behind them. "I think the men are almost ready for you."

Rebekah reached for him and pulled him into the hug with his wife. "I will never forget your kindness."

Ori chuckled. "We shall not forget you either, dear Rebekah."

She finally released them and turned to face the scene from which she wished to run.

Eliezer's caravan of ten camels had been reduced

to four. The men secured the few packs the group had managed to repair from the swords of the thieves. Ori and Zahar did their best to fill the pouches from their meager supplies and added a few more of their own sacks for extra measure.

Rebekah looked into the large eyes of the remaining camels and imagined their companions. They had not been lost to illness or famine, but bandits; men seeking their own gain at the cost of others. She shuddered. She had been close to sharing their fate.

Silence from the men was deafening as they focused on the tasks at hand and the only one left for them to accomplish; get her to her waiting bridegroom unharmed.

Ori called from the doorway, "Take care of our boy."

She glanced over her shoulder and smiled. "I shall do my best." Her gaze returned to the sight before her.

Hadiya and Deborah each sat atop a camel. The four men and Eliezer stood around them. One camel still knelt in the sand. Dov stood beside it waiting to assist her.

She took a deep breath and made her way toward him. With a gentle but firm hand, he helped her mount her ride. Once she settled, she gave a sharp nod to Eliezer. He commanded the camel to stand. Rebekah held on as the animal under her rose to its feet.

Ori and Zahar stood together leaning on each

other as they waved.

Rebekah bowed her head toward them as Eliezer turned her camel toward the city gates.

Without a word, the group marched out of Damascus and headed toward their next destination.

When Rebekah could no longer make out the jewel of Damascus behind her, nerves crawled their way up and down her skin. "How long before we reach Shechem?"

Eliezer kept his eyes on the distant horizon. "About a week."

A week? The thought brought new fear to Rebekah's already anxious mind and heart. What else would be waiting for them in the span of a week?

Chapter 15

"So Abraham called the name of that place, 'The LORD will provide'; as it is said to this day, 'On the mount of the LORD it shall be provided.' "
-Genesis 22:14

Shechem, 2025 B.C.
Rebekah

Despite fears and restless nights, one week later, Rebekah's camel spread his hefty toes on the banks of a ford of the Jordan River.

Eliezer carefully guided the lead camel down into the water as the rest followed.

The river was calm as the caravan made their way slowly across the shallows to the other side.

Once they were clear of the water, it was only a few hours of heading directly west before Rebekah found her gaze falling upon the gates of Shechem.

As she looked down, she noticed dark circles discolored the skin under the men's eyes as testament to their constant guard. Their shoulders threatened to droop if not for the constant rigidness they fought to maintain. Even the camels sagged under the strain of weight and quick pace.

Eliezer took the group into town and promptly purchased a room for the night.

Rebekah's gaze flowed to the men. "Don't you think we should make it two?"

Eliezer glanced in their direction. "I don't want any more delays. One good night's rest will do us all some good."

Once Eliezer was satisfied the camels were stalled, and their belongings were safely brought into their rented room, he pulled Rebekah aside. "I have something I want to show you."

Her eyes flicked to Hadiya and Deborah.

"We'll take Layth with us and leave the others together."

She nodded.

He notified the men of his plan and took Rebekah into the marketplace.

The three walked up the street until they came to the animal market. Eliezer stopped only to purchase a young lamb. Rebekah noticed that the collection of sheep was few and poor. The old servant had paid handsomely for the best the merchant had to offer. Layth hoisted the sheep onto his shoulder as they made their way out of the city.

The main gate opened to a wide plain filled with

groves of oak trees. One tree, in particular, stood out taller than the rest. It was overshadowed by an even taller structure that was very familiar to Rebekah.

The massive square building held seven levels, all painted in various colors surrounded by widening staircases that resembled the one in Haran.

Her gaze darted to Eliezer. "Why are you taking me to a temple?"

Eliezer's eyes were bright with a light she hadn't seen since they left his parent's house. "I'm not."

Rebekah took in the sight as they passed the building. Altars were adorned with various idols. Some she recognized and some were not familiar to her. It was rumored the Canaanites competed in number of gods with Ur. Some of the idols were dressed in robes and had bowls of food positioned at their feet. Priests' and priestesses' chants of praises and petitions floated on the air all around. Competing incenses clouded the open space and rose toward the sky in hopes the prayers attached would be heard.

Eliezer paused for a moment to look at the crowd. "People come to this place from all around seeking a vision from their deity." He waved toward the gathering. "It was here that Abraham first saw Elohim."

"You mean in a vision?"

"I mean in the flesh." He raised his eyebrows high. "Though he had heard Elohim's voice for some time, it was not until he reached Shechem that Elohim revealed Himself."

"Revealed himself… in flesh?"

He turned to continue, "I know it doesn't seem like a real possibility, but it's true. In this very place, Elohim made Himself known to Master Abraham."

"Did you see him?"

Eliezer connected with her gaze and nodded.

She watched the fire in his eyes blaze wildly.

He went a little further until they came to the massive oak and walked around it.

On the other side, in the canopies' shadow, stood a most curious sight. A pile of unhewn stones sat neatly arranged in the form of an altar. Unlike its towering counterpart, this altar stood completely bare. No idols cluttered its platform. No offerings were present. No priestesses chanted petitions before it.

"The stranger's voice Abraham followed became the physical shepherd guiding him into the land that was promised to him." Eliezer waved to the structure. "And so, he built this very altar to Elohim. A testament to the one true God. Abraham's first altar, but not his last."

Eliezer arranged a bundle of wood from nearby scattered branches on the altar. He motioned for the lamb from Layth and slit the animal's throat. Placing the lamb onto the altar, he lit a fire and lifted his hands to pray.

Rebekah put her hand on his arm. "What are you doing?"

"Praying."

"But you're not a priest." She looked around to see if the gathering of priests and priestesses were watching them.

"With Elohim, you don't have to be."

She kept her voice low, "If your god doesn't have an idol, how do you know he will hear you?"

"He is always ready to listen to those who call on Him."

She pulled her hand back.

Eliezer's deep voice rang clear and strong in the shade of the massive oak.

Rebekah felt as if she were listening in on a private conversation. His words were filled with joy, thanksgiving, and most of all hope. Her name crossed his lips more than once.

When he finished, he stood quietly watching the sacrifice burn.

Rebekah watched the fire, too. "How do you know what is an acceptable offering?"

"I've witnessed Master Abraham perform many an offering. Of course, none more important than the one he didn't make."

She perked up. "How can an offering be important if it's not made?"

Eliezer's eyes danced with the flames. "Several years ago, when we lived in a place in the Philistine's land Master Abraham called Beersheba, he came to me and told me to prepare a donkey. He told me we were taking a trip to the land of Moriah, about a three days journey away. Isaac was about your age at the time and he was to accompany us along with Layth." He looked to the man standing quietly next to them. "The four of us packed what supplies we needed and Abraham cut a bundle of wood and added it to our load. I had seen the preparation before. I knew we were going to make a sacrifice. I just didn't know why we were leaving home to do it."

"Abraham didn't tell you?"

He shook his head. "I knew he had heard from Elohim." He smiled. "He would always get this look on his face."

"Fear?"

"Determination. Like he knew what needed to be done and nothing was going to stand in the way of his obedience." He looked to her for a moment before returning his gaze to the flames. "The four of us headed out. It was a normal journey. Just four men walking…talking…then when we made it to the mountain in Moriah, Abraham told Layth and me to wait at the foot of the mountain. Only he and Isaac would be going further to worship and that they both would be returning. He untied the bundle of wood and laid it across Isaac's strong shoulders. He took the kindling for a fire and a knife in his hand. Then the two of them disappeared up the mountain."

He quieted as he watched the smoke rise.

"What happened?"

"I didn't find out until later, but I had found it odd." He rubbed his chin.

"What?"

"That we didn't bring a lamb or goat or even a calf with us for the offering." He turned to her. "When the two of them came back, there was a heavy silence between them as if something unexpected had happened. Isaac didn't speak to his father for the rest of the journey back. It wasn't until we returned home that Abraham confided in me about what happened on that mountain."

"What did he tell you?"

"As they were climbing, Isaac asked regarding the offering. Abraham told him that Elohim would provide. When they got to the place Elohim had told Abraham, he built an altar there and prepared to make a sacrifice."

"But they still didn't have the offering."

"But they did."

Rebekah scrunched her brow. "It was only the two of them. They didn't bring any animal with them or hunt."

"What we didn't know is that Abraham had brought the intended sacrifice with him."

Rebekah thought for a few moments. When the idea entered her mind, a tremor rushed up the middle of her back causing her to shiver. The name floated over her lips, "Isaac?"

He slowly nodded.

"Elohim asked Abraham to sacrifice his own son?"

His distant gaze returned to the burning offering.

"But I don't understand. I'm supposed to be Isaac's bride. Why are you bringing me to a dead bridegroom?"

"I'm not. He is alive and waiting for you."

"I don't understand."

"I didn't at first either." He chuckled. "After Abraham built the altar, he bound Isaac and helped the young man lay on the wood. Isaac refused to speak of that day, so I don't have any idea what was going on in his mind, but when Abraham recounted the story to me, he was trembling. He told me he took the knife and held it up to Isaac's throat. He was about to make the fatal cut when he heard a voice call out his name.

"When he realized it was Elohim, he said he burst into tears. He nearly did the same telling me. Elohim told him not to finish the sacrifice because the mere act of obedience had been sacrifice enough. Then Abraham noticed movement in a thicket nearby and realized a ram had gotten his horns stuck. He took the ram and sacrificed the animal instead of his son. He decided to call the place Yehovah Yireh, meaning Yehovah will provide for the need seen."

She put a hand on her hip. "And you all just returned home as if nothing happened?"

"For the most part." He shrugged. "Though I'm sorry to say that things were not the same between father and son from then on, nor husband and wife for that matter. Sarah and Isaac couldn't seem to understand Master Abraham's devotion to Elohim. The two retreated into each other and cautiously watched Abraham as if he would attempt to harm them at any moment. Life wasn't the same after that."

As they walked back to the city, Rebekah kept reliving the moments Isaac endured at the hands of his father. *How could Abraham willingly lay down his son on the altar of Elohim?* She'd heard stories of Canaanites offering their children up to the fires of their gods, but she thought Abraham's god was different. Perhaps he held the same bloodthirst all deities seemed to possess. Perhaps he wasn't so different after all.

Chapter 16

*"And Abraham lifted up his eyes and looked, and
behold, behind him was a ram, caught in a thicket by
his horns. And Abraham went and took the ram and
offered it up as a burnt offering instead of his son."*
-Genesis 22:13

Wilderness of Paran, 2025 B.C.
Isaac

Isaac stood on a mountain range in Paran watching his
flock graze on the sparse shrubs. His eyes were on his
sheep, but his thoughts were far away in another time,
on another mountain.

"Isaac?" Jedidiah's call brought him back to the
moment. "Don't you think we should press on?"

His focus sharpened on what lay before him. His
poor sheep had picked the area clean and were rooting
in the rocks for more. He shook his head. "I'm sorry,
let's keep moving."

"Where are you today?" The man leaned on his staff. "That's the third time you've seemed to freeze over."

Isaac again tried to shake away his wandering thoughts. "Must be the heat."

Jedidiah looked up into the sky. Though the sun was shining bright, the immense temperature of the day had not yet overtaken them. "What has really stolen your attention?" He lifted a bushy brow at his companion. "Perhaps an approaching bride?"

Isaac turned to look over his shoulder as if the woman Eliezer had gone to retrieve would appear there at any moment. He had imagined her a hundred times, but never having seen her, he didn't know what features her face would truly hold.

Since the news of Eliezer's departure reached him, days had turned to weeks and weeks had completed a full moon's cycle with more passing quickly. He knew the journey to be long, but with so many unknowns, the day his bride would finally arrive was a complete secret to him. He had to depend on Eliezer to find her, keep her from harm, and deliver her to himself. An almost impossible task for any man, but Isaac knew Eliezer. If anyone was going to be able to accomplish it, he was the man to do it.

Isaac sighed. "If I'm being honest, my thoughts today have been on the past, not the future."

Jedidiah pressed off his staff and walked along the stony path. "The past can be a terrible trap for those who reside there too long." He allowed silence to hang while they walked. "What moment has you trapped?"

Isaac looked to the top of the ridge. "The mountain in Moriah."

Without any further words, the shepherd knew the day of which his manager spoke. Though he had not gone with Eliezer and Layth that day to the mountain, it was a day that was rarely addressed and one that changed the household of Abraham. He kept his lips sealed and prayed to Elohim that Isaac would not.

When they reached a patch of fresh pasture, Jedidiah stood beside Isaac and watched the sheep graze.

Isaac's eyes lifted to the mountain top. "I've relived that day so many times, but I still can't believe what my father almost did."

Jedidiah kept silent. He knew Isaac to be a man of few words, but more flowed if one remained patient enough.

"When I realized his intention, the moment he held out that rope to me, my whole view of him shattered. Don't get me wrong, I heard the talk of people. They believed my father to be of half a mind, but I always believed he was genuine in his belief in Elohim. I had grown up believing Elohim to be a kind deity who wanted to give us good things. One who had called my father into a land where he could thrive." He shook his head and let his gaze drop to his sandals.

"When I laid down on that altar and felt the poke

of sticks in my back, the tight rub of the rope on my wrists, and caught the sunlight reflecting off my father's knife, I felt the most helpless I had ever felt in my life." His attention came up. "I knew I wasn't. I knew myself to be stronger and faster than my aging father. It would have been nothing for me to overpower him."

"Why didn't you?"

Isaac's eyes widened. "When I saw the resolve in his eyes, I knew he had heard from Elohim. I knew my father wouldn't allow a single hair on my head to be moved without a word from his God. At that moment, I realized something…"

Jedidiah waited as he watched Isaac wrestle with his thoughts.

"…I realized that if Elohim had really called my father to sacrifice me, then my part was to obey. That if I refused, it meant disobedience on his part."

Jedidiah watched the sheep graze at their feet. "Well the way I see it, it's kind of like raising sheep here in the wilderness." He spread his arm out.

"What do you mean?"

"I mean, in other places they have lush green valleys filled with all the grass sheep could feed on, but not here. The rain falls so little that the only place we can find pasture is hidden in the rocks where the water collects."

"So?"

"So-o-o-o, that's what it's like with Elohim. Now,

I don't claim to be as smart as your father or Eliezer, but I do trust Elohim." He pulled at his chin in thought. "We are good shepherds, are we not?"

Isaac nodded.

"Because we bring our flocks out here and show them where to find grass, right?"

He nodded again.

"But they have to follow us every moment. They don't know where the grass is. We have to show them. But we don't just point out all the spots and leave them to wander around. We guide them to each patch as they need to feed. It's our job to make sure they have enough for every part of every day." He waited to see if Isaac was following.

Isaac's brows knitted together. "You're saying that Elohim only reveals a little at a time for what the person needs?"

"Exactly!" He slapped him on the back. "Your father didn't have all the answers the day he packed that donkey. He was only told to go, just like when he left Haran. When he got to the mountain, he was told to take only you. When he built the altar, he only knew Elohim had asked him to sacrifice you."

Jedidiah lifted his finger. "But he also knew that Elohim had promised you would be the one to start a new nation. In your father's mind, he believed both promise and request could only coexist if Elohim was the One who controlled the next steps. Abraham didn't know the exact path he was going to take that day, but he knew Elohim was a good shepherd leading him. It was his job to follow."

The conflicting ideas of obedience and bitterness raged inside Isaac. When his mother found out what happened on that mountain, she was furious. The mere thought of harm to him was too much for her. Isaac couldn't blame her. It had taken almost one hundred years for her to see the face of her only child and then his father had nearly ended that precious life in one trip. She couldn't move past the thought of Elohim taking him away from her.

Isaac had sided with his mother. They hadn't heard the voice of Elohim's call to go. They weren't told to build an altar and lay upon it. He looked up into his fellow shepherd's eyes. "How can you trust a god you don't hear from?"

"Because of His past actions." His smile widened. "When your father left Haran, what did he gain?"

"Land?"

"Does he own any?"

Isaac thought. "Only the cave in Machpelah."

"Alright, but land was only part of the promise. He gained you as well."

He nodded.

"When you both went up that mountain and you *both* came down again, what did your father gain?"

He shrugged.

"You—again, and a recounting of the original promise." Jedidiah poked Isaac's chest. " *You* were the one Elohim had chosen. Not Ishmael and not anyone else. You."

"Yet I stand here in the middle of a desert with no bride and no child to start this new nation." He waved his arms around for emphasis. "How am I supposed to follow a shepherd who tried to kill me?"

"But He didn't. His request was for your father's release of you. We so easily hold on to blessings given to us that they often become our new focus. Elohim called Abraham to let go of you, and He called you to take hold of Him."

The idea weighed down on Isaac, pressing his shoulders inward.

"Our sheep don't wake up every morning wondering if they are going to follow us that day." Jedidiah pointed to the flock. "They follow us today because we filled their needs yesterday and the day before that.

"Elohim is asking you to follow Him one day at a time because He has been faithful every day past." He put a hand on Isaac's shoulder. "Don't you see? That day was never meant to end with your death. Elohim already had that ram waiting as a substitute sacrifice for you. But just as your father had to surrender you, you must surrender you. That day on the hill was the beginning of life." He released his grip and shook his head. "All I'm trying to say is that if Elohim can be God with your father in the promised land, He can be God with us in this wilderness."

Isaac straightened his back and squared his shoulders with the new perspective.

Jedidiah met his master's gaze and held it. "Your bride is coming, and your life's path is being unfolded before your very eyes. But you will only thrive if you follow Elohim with each and every footstep. In doing so, your bride will follow Elohim and so will your children and your children's children. Each one walking in the footprints you leave behind. Will they be toward Elohim or away from Him?"

Staring into the deep eyes of his companion, Isaac felt something stir inside. He couldn't put a name to the feeling, but it was as if something was pulling him. As if something was calling him. He didn't hear a voice, but he knew his Shepherd was making Himself known.

Chapter 17

"Sarah lived 127 years; these were the years of the life of Sarah. And Sarah died at Kiriath-arba (that is, Hebron) in the land of Canaan, and Abraham went in to mourn for Sarah and to weep for her."
-Genesis 23:1-2

Hebron, 2025 B.C.
Rebekah

Rebekah and her companions stayed one night within the gates of Shechem. The following days were spent staying close to the cities along the way south toward their next destination.

She knew the world to be a much larger place than she had ever experienced, but the past months had left her feeling as if the horizon would continue on forever. When could she put her tent stakes into the sands for more than one night?

In the distance, a small town came into view. Instead of turning toward it, Eliezer pointed the lead camel to a small field.

Rebekah lifted. "Where are we headed?"

"We have a stop to make before heading into Hebron."

At the end of the field stood a cave with a large boulder enclosing the mouth.

Eliezer gave Rebekah's camel the command to kneel. Once the animal settled, he extended his hand to her.

She accepted the aid and slid off the camel's back onto the rich soil which gave way slightly under her sandals.

The older man stood staring at the cave.

Rebekah looked to the boulder, then over her shoulder at the rest of her guard.

The other four men stood silently in reverence to something of which she was unaware.

"Where have you brought me?"

"Machpelah." He put a hand on the boulder. "This is the only land my master owns, and he used it to bury Sarah."

"Great *Doda* Sarah?" Rebekah took a step back and put her hands on her chest. She couldn't believe she was standing at the grave of her mother-in-law. "My family never received word of her passing."

Eliezer nodded slowly. "I thought of relaying the news when I came to find a bride for Isaac, but it just didn't seem like the appropriate time."

"I can't believe she's gone."

"She's actually the reason you're here."

Rebekah's attention came up. "I don't understand. What does her death have to do with me?"

"When Sarah fell ill, Abraham took a concubine by the name of Keturah. When Sarah died, Abraham buried her here and took Keturah as his new wife. This did not please Isaac. Who could blame him?" He shrugged. "Master Abraham was on his second wife, and he hadn't found one for his only son."

She shook her head. "I still don't understand what that has to do with me."

"Seeing Isaac upset over the new union, Abraham finally realized what he was withholding from Isaac and sent me on my mission to find a wife for his son."

"You're saying that if Sarah hadn't died, you wouldn't have come for me?"

"Possibly." He turned back to the cave. "Maybe at some point Abraham would have sent me."

Rebekah took a few steps forward and placed her hand on the cool stone. "I wish I had gotten the chance to meet her."

"Oh, you would have loved her." He smiled. "I think she would have favored you as well."

"You think so?"

Eliezer laughed. "That woman had the dignity and grace of a princess and the spirit of a raging fire all wrapped up in one of the most beautiful women I've ever had the pleasure of knowing." He sighed. "Poor Isaac took her death hard."

Her breath caught in her throat. *Isaac.* The man had lost his mother and watched his father marry another woman before finding him a bride. Rebekah thought back to her father and the pain of loss scratched at her healing wounds. *How Isaac must be aching too.*

"Well," Eliezer turned slowly, "we should be heading into Hebron. I'm sure Master Abraham will be excited to see us.

Rebekah mounted her camel, and the group rode away from the cave.

A short distance to the south and around a ridge, a massive city came into view on a distant hill. The hewn-stone walls displayed the occupants' clear ability to defend themselves.

Eliezer paused.

Rebekah stretched to see. "Have we arrived?"

He looked up at her. "At Hebron, yes. This is where Master Abraham resides with Keturah. We shall go to him first."

"What of Isaac?" She looked to the intimidating city. "Does he not reside here as well?"

He smiled and looked back at the stone walls. "I shall take you to him once we've gone to see my master."

The caravan made their way up the slopes.

From the height, Rebekah could see the land slope rapidly to the east, but it was more gradual to the west and south.

They passed through the market street. Stalls were filled with fresh fruits piled as tall as Rebekah. She didn't wonder at the vast offerings with as rich as the soil at the nearby field seemed to be.

When they reached the animal market, a man stood tall and strong among a pen of sheep.

"Master Abraham." Eliezer ran to embrace the man. "I have completed the task you sent me to accomplish. I've brought a strong wife for your son."

"Well done, my good and faithful servant." Abraham smiled and patted Eliezer's back.

Eliezer gave the command for Rebekah's camel to kneel and held out his hand to assist her down.

Rebekah slid off the camel's back and bowed deeply.

Abraham returned the greeting. "And who do we have here?"

Rebekah felt her throat dry out. "I am Rebekah, daughter of Bethuel, which Milcah did bear to Nahor."

"Nahor?" Abraham's eyes widened. "You're Bethuel's daughter?"

"I am."

He patted Eliezer's shoulder harder. "Well done indeed. Truly Elohim has blessed your journey. This woman is of my own kin." His smile widened to reveal all his teeth. "How is Bethuel?"

She swallowed a rising lump in her throat. "He passed away from injuries sustained during a leopard attack last year."

"I'm sorry to hear that." He shrunk inward some. "I'm very sorry for your loss. Though as long as I have lived, I've learned that it is our struggles that make us strong."

Rebekah pushed down the memories of her father that threatened to send her away in tears. She took a breath. "This is my nurse, Deborah, and my handmaid, Hadiya." She waved to each woman in turn.

Abraham looked over the guard. "It appears you have all arrived safely." He straightened his shoulders and clapped. "Come, we must feast our new family member, and you must tell me of your trip."

Eliezer hesitated. "I'm afraid it's not all good news."

Abraham paused.

"We were ambushed during our journey, and we sustained the loss of some of your camels and provisions."

"I see." The older man tugged at his long, gray beard for some time.

Rebekah thought back to the dreaded day she had pressed from her mind. The camels and cargo weren't the only things they had lost. Her faithful companion, Zami, now rested from his work in the field of Eliezer's parents. Tears burned at her eyes, but she blinked them away.

Abraham smoothed down his beard. "Camels and coins can be replaced." He moved through the flock toward the door to let himself and Eliezer out.

Rebekah turned her attention to the animals. Her heart ached for her own sheep. She wondered if they had learned to follow Laban in the time she had been gone. Something about the ones in the stall in front of her seemed familiar. "You raise sheep?"

"Best flocks this side of the Jordan." He set the latch firmly in place. "These Canaanites think sheep weak and much prefer their sturdy goats." He scoffed. "I've been able to persuade them to fancy our sheep from Ur." He gave her a wink.

Sheep from Ur. That's why they looked so familiar to her. She had forgotten that when Abraham left Haran, he took his flocks with him. These sheep were kin to the ones she raised with her family.

"My success seems to get me in trouble with family though." He chuckled. "First, my kin in Haran and then Lot right here in Hebron. The more Elohim blesses, the more I've got to manage."

He led them out of the walled city toward a group of tents so far spread that it could pass as its own town.

At the door of the largest tent, a beautiful woman stood waiting. The wind whipped her hair and the fresh scent of sweet calamus floated on the breeze to Rebekah. It was at that moment, she realized how much she must smell like the stench of men and travel. What kind of impression was she going to make on her new mother-in-law?

The woman's darker skin set a perfect background for glittering jewelry that adorned her neck, ears, and arms. She watched with a hopeful gaze as Abraham neared.

"Greetings, wife." Abraham kissed both of her cheeks. "I'd like to introduce you to Isaac's bride, Rebekah." He waved toward her.

Rebekah bowed reverently.

Keturah held a bright smile. "Greetings, Rebekah. I'm happy to see you have arrived. We've been expecting you for some time."

Eliezer appeared beside her. "Our journey has been a long one."

"I, for one, can't wait to hear all about it." Abraham practically bounced near them. "Keturah, would you have the servants start making preparations. Tonight, we shall feast in honor of our new daughter, Rebekah."

"Of course, my lord." She fought a wrinkle in her nose. "But I should also see to it that the women have a chance to make themselves more… presentable."

Abraham furrowed his brow.

Keturah motioned to the women with a slight nod of her head.

"Oh." He caught her meaning. "Where are my manners? Of course, of course. We shall have all the resources at your disposal to refresh yourselves before the meal is ready."

"You are most kind, Great *Dod* Abraham." Rebekah bowed.

"I shall see to the men." Eliezer directed the guards away to another tent.

Keturah used her finger to motion Rebekah to follow her into the tent behind her.

She obeyed and waved Hadiya and Deborah to accompany her.

Inside, Rebekah noticed the huge tent was divided into several rooms. Voices filled the hidden spaces.

Keturah stood in the large open space. "Jora."

A young woman appeared from behind one of the dividing curtains. "Yes, Mistress?"

"Would you begin preparations? Eliezer has returned with Isaac's bride, and Abraham has ordered a feast tonight to celebrate."

"Right away, my mistress." The woman ducked back behind the curtain.

"Now then," Keturah turned to appraise Rebekah, "let's see to it that you are properly tended for tonight. Do you have something a bit less…"

"Travel attire?" Rebekah offered.

She dipped her chin slightly. "Well, yes."

"I'm not sure." Rebekah looked down at the simple dress Zahar had placed in a sack. "You see our caravan was ambushed and—"

"Ambushed!" Keturah covered her mouth. "You poor dear. Well, never mind. Don't you worry. I'm sure we can find you something suitable." She looked around Rebekah. "And who do you have with you?"

"My apologies." Rebekah blushed. "This is my nurse, Deborah, and my handmaid, Hadiya."

"I'm sure we can find suitable garments for them

as well." She smiled faintly at the two women. "When Abraham has a feast, it is a true feast. We shall all want to look our very best." She paused to look Rebekah up and down again before her gaze returned to the two servants. She stroked her throat with a grimace. "I think we shall start with a bath. I'll have some fresh water drawn."

As Abraham's servants worked the rest of the day to prepare the meal, Keturah readied Rebekah. She rubbed her down with lotions and herbs, painted her face with powders, then brushed and braided her hair to perfection. Lastly, she adorned her with jewelry from head to toe.

Rebekah felt the weight of the gems. "I think this is too much."

"It is never enough." Keturah set another bracelet on her arm. "Why Abraham ever sent that servant of his halfway across the world to pick a bride when there are plenty of decent women around here is beyond me. All I know is that you have been chosen, and I must do everything in my power to prepare you for what lies ahead. I may not have given birth to Isaac, but I view him as a son. He deserves the very best we can offer."

When the women were ready and the meal was set, Keturah took Rebekah to the feast.

The gathering of servants and shepherds all watched Rebekah as she was guided to Abraham. Her skin crawled as all eyes watched her every movement. The feeling of being the center of attention was one she was not used to and didn't want to get used to. What kind of life had she agreed to? Flowing dresses and trinkets of gold were not what she imagined her future would hold.

Eliezer stood waiting for her. He took her hand and walked her closer to Abraham. "My master, may I present to you Rebekah, daughter of Bethuel, the betrothed of Isaac."

At the mention of her father's name, Rebekah's heart thudded. How she wished he could see her today. Would he be proud of the choices that led her to this moment? Would he beam with pride next to her mother, brother, and the rest of her extended family? She wanted them all there to celebrate with her, but they were so far away. She blinked back tears that threatened to displace hours of Keturah's hard work.

Abraham gently took Rebekah's hand in his. "My daughter, may you be blessed of Elohim. May you be the mother of ten thousands and a good wife to my son."

The gathering erupted in cheers and shouts of joy.

Rebekah jumped from the noise.

Abraham chuckled. "We feast in her honor tonight before we send her off to Isaac. Please," he waved to the crowd, "enjoy!"

The people wasted no time in devouring the prepared foods and drinking in the merriment.

Rebekah sat with Abraham and Keturah, barely picking at the platters offered to her. She kept her gaze lowered, for every time she looked up someone else was staring at her. She knew they meant no harm in their glances, but she felt embarrassed all the same.

Late into the night, when the wine flowed free, she was finally able to be excused to rest.

Jora accompanied Rebekah and her women to Keturah's tent where she showed her where they could sleep.

Rebekah laid down and huddled close to Hadiya and Deborah. She knew deep down that this would be one of the last nights she had to sleep beside them. Once her marriage to Isaac was complete, she would lie with him for all her days.

She breathed in their earthy, feminine scents trying to capture them in her memories while she listened to the sounds of her wedding feast echo in the fields.

Chapter 18

"Abraham planted a tamarisk tree in Beersheba and called there on the name of the LORD, the Everlasting God."
-Genesis 21:33

Beersheba, 2025 B.C.
Rebekah

Rebekah awoke to the bright sun's rays attempting to reach into the tent. She blinked several times and stared up at a tent ceiling that didn't belong to her. Movement next to her head caused Rebekah to turn and see Keturah standing over her.

"Rise, daughter of Bethuel." The woman had her hands folded across her chest and her sandaled foot tapped out an impatient beat. "Abraham has sent for you."

Rebekah sat up and looked around for the dress she had worn on her travel.

"If you are searching for that filthy rag, I've had it

disposed of." She flicked her fingers to one side. "There is a pile of garments over there that you may choose from." She turned and disappeared behind the curtain.

A lump rose in Rebekah's throat. One of the precious dresses from Zahra was no more. The woman who had nestled herself so deeply and so quickly into Rebekah's heart had offered up the little she had to a stranger.

Tears stung her eyes. She couldn't be angry with Keturah. There was no way for her to know what the garment meant to Rebekah. With the days of hard travel, she was sure its thick layer of sand and dirt and the deep odor of sweat would repel such a dainty flower adorned with gems like Keturah. This life was certainly much different than what Rebekah knew.

She hurried to change out of the elegant dress and into one a bit less formal accompanied with a simple wrap that she draped across her shoulders. With a nearby rag, she wiped off the remnants of her makeup and adjusted her hair as best she could without the aid of a bronze mirror. When she felt satisfied, she stepped out of the backroom into the main part of the massive tent.

Keturah waited by the door. She clicked her tongue at the sight of Rebekah. "Here, let me fix your hair." She moved to adjust the pieces of partial braids that had come loose with Rebekah's tossing in her sleep.

Rebekah flushed under her hands.

She stepped back to observe her. "Well, that's the best we can do for now. We don't want to keep Abraham waiting any longer."

She nodded and followed her out of the tent.

Abraham stood beside Eliezer and three packed camels.

Deborah and Hadiya were already mounted on their camels while the lead animal remained empty.

Layth and Dov were adjusting the straps of the cargo.

Rebekah made her way quietly to the group.

"I pray this day finds you well, dear child." Abraham's smile was broad and his eyes were bright.

She nodded. "Are we leaving so soon?"

"I am going to escort you to Beersheba, but from there you will go on to meet Isaac without me. I'm afraid my son and I are not on the best of terms right now."

Sadness pulled at her heart as she watched some of the brightness leave Abraham's countenance.

Dov held out his hand to help her up.

Rebekah mounted the camel she had rode all the way from Haran. The beast lifted and marched under her as if his only duty in life was to carry her over the sands for all time.

Abraham led the caravan. "Eliezer told me of your ambush." He snuck a quick peek up at her before returning his eyes to the horizon. "I do apologize.

Perhaps I should have sent more guards to escort you."

Rebekah looked down at Layth and Dov as they flanked her. "The men defended us with every ounce of their strength. I fear even if we had a hundred men, those bandits would have attempted to raid us."

"Still. I'm so glad Elohim protected you."

Eliezer smiled up at Rebekah from behind Abraham. "Me too."

Rebekah enjoyed the cool breeze of morning as it played with her hair. She felt free from the burden of heavy jewelry and elegant garments purchased from distant lands. The comfortable feel of linen and wool next to her skin was a welcomed one. They reminded her of the fields and her family. Even her face felt unburdened with the removal of the thick mask of makeup.

The day of travel was filled with Eliezer and the men sharing stories of their journey with Abraham. Rebekah added a few comments here and there, but mostly allowed the men to talk amongst themselves.

Just before nightfall, they came upon the small city of Beersheba.

Abraham guided them outside the city to a grove of tamarisk trees.

Rebekah noticed their smooth reddish-brown bark and the blush of their pink flowers blowing in the wind.

Layth helped Rebekah off her camel, and she walked with Abraham in the grove.

Abraham stopped and put his hand on the tallest

tree. "I planted this grove when I first arrived in Beersheba." He patted the trunk. "This is where I called on El 'Olam, the everlasting God."

Rebekah looked up into the wide canopy. "You have many names for your one god. Eliezer has shared many with me in his stories."

"I would expect nothing less of my servant." Abraham glanced at Eliezer. "Even if Eliezer were not trying to prepare you, he would have told you of the God he serves anyway. When you are devoted to something, you can't help but share it."

She turned to face him. "Why trade so many gods for one with so many names?"

His smile broadened until it lit up his whole face. "The truth is, our God has many names because He reveals Himself in so many ways."

She took a few steps deeper into the grove. "You know my family used to tell the story of Inanna and her Huluppu tree."

He nodded. "I'm familiar with the story."

"It used to be my favorite." She remembered the laughter and joy shared around the tables with her family. Then the reminder of how very far away they were stole her happiness. The loss of her father came crashing down on her afresh.

"Used to?"

She nodded, desperately trying to fight back her tears. "When my father got sick, I prayed to Inanna. I begged her to restore him back to us." Tears streamed down her face as she tried to blink them away. "She didn't listen."

He leaned on the tree between them. "Idols are deaf and blind to our prayers."

She chuckled despite her sorrow. "I found that out too late."

"It's never too late to realize the truth."

"Truth." The word felt foreign on her tongue. "I don't think anyone really knows truth."

"Elohim does because He is."

She met his steady gaze. "How can you be so sure?"

"I've heard His call, I've seen Him face to face, and I've been on the receiving end of His many fulfilled promises." He shrugged. "How could I not be sure?"

She shook her head.

He bent down and gathered a handful of sand. "As you get older, time runs faster like sand through open fingers." He spread his fingers allowing some of the sand to run out. "Make the most of each grain you're given." He reached out for her hand.

She held it open to him.

Abraham poured the sand into her cupped hand. "Once they're gone, you don't get any more."

Rebekah felt the grains run through her fingers.

"No one is forcing you to believe in Elohim. Not even Elohim forces Himself on anyone. But the longer you wait to follow Him, the more you sink into the sands of your own making. He is waiting to plant you in fertile soil so you can thrive."

She felt the coarse grains against her palms. "Do you think Elohim made a mistake in choosing me?"

Abraham smiled. "I believe He answered the prayer of my servant, of me, and of Isaac. You are the one He has chosen. You are the one who will bring forth the promised blessing."

Rebekah looked down at the sand running through her fingers. The days of travel would soon be over for her and she would finally meet her betrothed. Suddenly, time seemed to be running much faster than she wanted.

Chapter 19

"And Isaac went out to meditate in the field toward evening. And he lifted up his eyes and saw, and behold, there were camels coming."
-Genesis 24:63

Beerlahairoi, 2025 B.C.
Isaac

Isaac lifted up a handful of dirt and allowed the rich soil to run through his fingers. The cool of approaching evening was a welcome reprieve from the overwhelming heat of the day. The sheep followed him contently to the new patch of grass he had found for them. While they munched happily on the last provision of the day, he set his gaze to the north. "It's been too long."

Jedidiah stood nearby. "It hasn't been that long."

"The moon completed its third cycle days ago." He stood and brushed the dirt off his hands. "What if something happened? Maybe I should send someone."

"If you send someone now and they miss the caravan along the way or something happens to them, what will it profit you?"

"You're right." He sighed and ran his long fingers through his hair. "I just don't know how much more of this waiting I can take."

"Maybe it's good that it's taking so long."

Isaac glared at him.

"Don't look at me like that." He leaned on his staff. "All I'm saying is that maybe Elohim is trying to use this season of waiting to work on you."

"What is that supposed to mean?"

"Why not have a little faith in Elohim like your father?"

He cut his eyes at his companion.

Jedidiah put his hands up with his palms out. "He has to be your God too. The faith of your father doesn't do any good if you don't have faith in Elohim yourself."

Isaac ruminated on his words and hung his head.

The younger shepherd drove the flocks toward their camp leaving Isaac.

With a slow and steady gait, Isaac walked down the mountainside and into the open fields. He looked up into the clear sky. *I know You want me to surrender, Elohim, but it's not easy. I have so many questions. There are so many things that don't make any sense. I do want You to be my God. I just don't know how to have faith like Abba. He trusts You so completely. But*

I guess it's easy when one can hear and see You. You've never so much as whispered to me. How am I supposed to follow where I can't see?

He paused and dropped his gaze. *Help me trust You. Help me learn to follow You as a good sheep would follow his shepherd. Keep my bride safe from harm. Bring her to me when You are ready.*

He lifted his eyes and noticed a dust cloud in the distance. He rushed toward the tents and saw the distinct outline of a caravan heading in their direction. "Camels?"

Jedidiah met him on the path. "Do you think it's her?"

A tremor went through Isaac. His throat became too dry to speak.

As the line of camels came into view, the face of his father's servant became clear as he led the pack closer. Three women sat atop three camels. One of them had to be her. One of them was his bride finally coming to be his.

Chapter 20

*"And Rebekah lifted up her eyes, and when she saw
Isaac, she dismounted from the camel"
-Genesis 24:64*

Beerlahairoi, 2025 B.C.
Rebekah

Rebekah noticed the land around them shift. The
sandy soil became fertile, perfect for grazing. To the
west, the sun was setting behind a distant mountain.

Her eyes beheld a most welcomed sight. Large
flocks of sheep dotted the land. It made her heart soar
to see the familiar scene.

Two shepherds stood near tents watching their
approach.

Her next thought struck like lightning through
her. *One of them must be Isaac.* She felt heat rise in
her cheeks and became dizzy. There would be no time
to prepare to meet her betrothed. The days of her
journey were finally at an end. She was moments away

from laying eyes on her bridegroom.

Acting quickly, she drew her wrap up over her head and pulled one end to her face to cover her nose and mouth, leaving only her eyes unveiled.

Eliezer pushed the camels faster. "There waits Isaac. No doubt he has counted the sunsets until your arrival." He gave her a backward glance.

When they were about a stone's throw away from the men, Eliezer gave the command for the camels to halt and kneel.

Dov helped Rebekah dismount.

Deborah and Hadiya dismounted as well and stood behind Rebekah. Their quiet show of support kept her on her feet because her knees felt as if they would give out with the next strong breeze.

The two men approached them.

"Greetings, Master Isaac." Eliezer bowed deeply.

"Greetings."

Rebekah's gaze took in Isaac. His voice was deep and reverberated through her. His strong features resembled his father, but he held the distinct handsomeness of his youth. Two hazel eyes sparkled back at her under dark brows. Thick, almost wavy black hair hung just slightly around his face. His rich skin was kissed by the sun revealing to her that he had spent much of his life outside. Her breath failed to maintain a normal rhythm. She had pictured a plain man with whom she was expected to spend her days. Never had she imagined he would be so striking.

Isaac looked to each of the people standing before him. "I trust your journey was a pleasant one."

Eliezer hesitated. "A successful one." He glanced toward Rebekah without making eye contact. "May I present to my master his bride, Rebekah."

Rebekah bowed low. When her eyes lifted, she found Isaac staring at her. It was a good thing she had covered her face because, with as much heat as she could feel under her covering, she was sure her cheeks were nearing the color of sumac berries.

Isaac shook his head as if he were trying to shake away a dream. "Layth. Dov. It is good to see you well."

The two guards bowed, but held their tongues.

"And who else do we have here?" He looked around Rebekah to the two women standing as still as statues. "I believe my father only sent for one wife, not three." A small smile played at the edges of his lips.

"My apologies, Master." Eliezer waved to the women. "These are Rebekah's nurse, Deborah, and her handmaiden, Hadiya."

"I see." He appraised the women with thoughtful eyes.

"We have been to see Master Abraham." The old servant waved to the north. "He sends his blessing."

Isaac nodded. "I'm sure he does."

Eliezer glanced at Rebekah before turning back to Isaac. "I must take my leave."

"So soon?" Isaac protested. "You only just arrived, and night is falling. It is no time to travel."

"The men and I will be fine." He motioned to the guards. "Abraham has need of me in Hebron now that I have safely delivered Rebekah to you."

The two men unloaded the few packs and set them beside Jedidiah.

Eliezer passed Rebekah with a wink.

She couldn't restrain herself for one more moment. She lunged out to him with open arms and embraced him. "Thank you," she whispered into his gray hair. "For everything."

He hugged her tight. "In life, we take many journeys. It is just that ours together is complete." He held her out to arm's length. "Remember what I shared with you, and may Elohim bless you, sweet child."

She released him too soon and turned to watch him direct the three camels away. When they disappeared down the path, she turned back to face Isaac.

He stood patiently waiting. "Eliezer is a good man."

She nodded; her mouth unable to form words under his intense gaze.

He looked at his companion. "This is Jedidiah. My fellow shepherd and hired hand."

Jedidiah bowed to the women. "A pleasure."

"Would you see to it the women have a place to sleep tonight?" He looked back at Rebekah. "I'm sorry we are not better prepared. We had no warning of when you would arrive."

"They can have my tent for the night." Jedidiah

smiled. "I don't mind sleeping among the sheep."

"That's very gracious, friend. We can work out more details tomorrow." He waved to the women. "Ladies, if you'll follow Jedidiah, he'll show you where you can rest."

Jedidiah scooped up two of the sacks. "This way."

Deborah and Hadiya collected the remaining satchels and followed him to the tent.

Rebekah stood frozen to the ground.

Isaac turned back to her. He held out his hand. "Forgive me. I don't really know the expectations of formalities. I'm sure this is not how it is done in your culture."

She shook her head.

"It's not really like this normally for us either. I'm sorry you won't have a wedding feast."

"Your father actually held one the other night for me," her voice was tight and strained.

"I'm sorry I missed the celebration." His smile beamed so bright, he appeared as playful as a child.

She grinned behind her veil.

A large dog bound up to Rebekah, nearly knocking her down.

Isaac pulled the beast back. "I'm so sorry about Tira. She's not accustomed to sharing me."

The massive dog panted heavy. Her tan fur and golden eyes shone in the evening light.

Rebekah's eyes watered. The face of her lost Zami filled her blurred vision.

Isaac looked up at her. "Are you harmed? She didn't mean—"

"No." She held up a hand. "I'm fine. She didn't hurt me. It's just…" She cleared her throat and blinked away the tears. "What's her breed?"

"She's the finest Kangal in all Canaan."

"A Kangal?" Rebekah's eyes burned.

"I raise them."

Large tears poured down her dusty cheeks and she was glad that most of her face was covered. "You raise them?" She looked up to see many more wandering among the flocks.

"Do you like Kangals?"

She smiled. "They are my favorite. My family had them for our flocks."

He rubbed Tira's head and rose. "Would you like to meet the rest of them?"

Rebekah saw his hazel eyes reflect the dimming sunlight like pools of warm honey. He stared back at her in gentleness with a hint of longing. Feelings she had never experienced suddenly awakened in her. "I would like that very much."

Chapter 21

"Then Isaac brought her into the tent of Sarah his mother and took Rebekah, and she became his wife, and he loved her. So Isaac was comforted after his mother's death."
-Genesis 24:67

Beerlahairoi, 2025 B.C.
Isaac

Isaac guided Rebekah into a makeshift pen. A group of large-pawed Kangal pups scurried toward him. He sat on the ground allowing the young dogs to lick at his face and tug at his tunic.

Rebekah stood nearby watching them play.

"These are from my latest litter." He patted the nearest puppy's head causing his large ears to flop back and forth. "Tira's litter."

"They're beautiful." Two puppies broke from the pack and came to play at her feet. She knelt close to them.

As they licked her with their rough tongues and playfully pawed at her, Isaac watched sorrow fill her eyes until they overflowed with fresh tears. The strange reaction was too much for him to bear. "Would you like one?"

Her attention came up. "What did you say?"

"I'll give you first choice."

She tilted her head. "First choice?"

"I promised my brother one, but I'll let you choose one of your very own."

Overcome with conflicting emotions, she tucked her chin.

"You don't want one?"

"It's not that." She looked up into his soft eyes. "It's that I was thinking about when I first got my Kangal, Zami."

He smiled. "If he meant that much to you, why didn't you bring him?"

"I did." She hesitated as she watched his interest focus. "I lost him on the journey."

Isaac's heart thudded against his ribs as he watched a dark sadness roll over Rebekah's eyes. "Would you mind if I asked how?"

She shook her head. "We were ambushed before reaching Damascus. Bandits killed some of your father's camels, stole our supplies, and tried to…" her voice caught in her throat, "tried to…"

He waited for her to clear her throat and continue.

"One of them had a hold of me." She rubbed her

wrist. "Zami came out of nowhere and leapt at the man." She put a hand to her neck. "They wrestled for some time. Zami had a hold of the man's throat, but the thief pierced his side with a sword."

Isaac moved closer to her. He wanted nothing more than to wrap her in his arms and assure her she was safe. Though knowing nothing about her and not wanting to frighten her, he kept some distance between them.

"We managed to get Zami to Damascus, but I'm afraid his wound was too great. Eliezer's father buried him in their field." She looked at Isaac. Large tears streamed down her face and spread through the material of her veil.

"I am so sorry." He reached for her and placed a gentle hand on hers. "I'm sure he was an amazing companion."

"The best." She smiled. "He was my protector, my best friend, and my fellow laborer in the wilderness. He meant everything to me."

Isaac thought for several moments, allowing the pack of puppies to play around them. "I know offering a replacement doesn't take away the pain, but they might provide you with comfort."

"Maybe." She stroked the nearest puppy's back.

His own words resounded in his mind. Images of his father's wedding feast filled his thoughts. That's what Eliezer had been trying to tell him. His father wasn't trying to replace his mother. He was simply looking for companionship in his pain. He shook his head with a heavy sigh. *How could I have been so thoughtless?*

He looked up into her dark eyes. "Choose any one you'd like."

Rebekah scanned the group. Each one was more beautiful than the last. They all had strong builds and were not afraid to play.

She picked one and held her up. "Who is this beauty?"

"Hava. She's the female most like her mother."

Rebekah inspected the girl. The truth was she could find nothing lacking in any of the dogs circling her. She decided Isaac must be very good at breeding indeed. "You name them?"

"And my sheep too." His cheeks flushed for a brief moment. "Jedidiah gives me much grief over it."

Rebekah paused. "You name your sheep?"

"Don't tell me you're going to give me grief over it too."

"No." She held up her hand. "I think it's wonderful. I name my sheep too. Well," she hesitated, "I used to name my sheep."

"Your sheep?" He tilted his head. "You mean your father's sheep."

"Oh no, I mean mine." Her smile broadened. "I was a shepherdess right alongside my father and my *dods*."

"They let you raise sheep?"

She chuckled. "There was no letting me about it. It's what I love to do."

"Oh, you mean when the men were home, you helped."

"No." She shook her head. "I went with my sheep up into the tablelands, crossed deserts and valleys, slept in the wilderness." She tucked her puppy close and stroked her head. "Everything."

He widened his gaze on her. "Everything?"

"Everything."

He shook his head and rubbed the back of his neck. "Can't say I've ever met a shepherdess before."

"Well, you have now." The puppy in her arms yawned. "I think I like her."

"Well, if you fancy her, then she's yours."

Rebekah hugged the girl.

"Come," he held out his hand to her, "take a walk with me."

She set down her new dog and took his hand. His skin was warm and welcoming.

They walked among the flocks in the last rays of the setting sun.

Jedidiah was preparing a small camp in the field for himself.

Rebekah watched him for a few moments before her attention turned toward two dogs circling the flock. "You have so many dogs. Do you keep all that you breed?"

"I try to keep as many as I can." He smiled

watching them walk. "If I could, I'd keep all of them simply because I love their company."

She smiled. At least she and this stranger-husband of hers had one thing in common.

"I try to hold onto enough to keep the breeding varied and so they can work in pairs."

"Pairs?"

"Yes, just as Elohim set all things in pairs in the garden, my dogs work better with a partner." He pointed out a large male. "Each protects in their own way. One may enjoy more sentinel work of constant rounds while another may enjoy staying closer to the flock. One may only go as far as the flock, but no further while another will go as far as it takes to make his point." He waved to each of the different dogs. "By understanding their preferences and pairing them, the flock benefits from their strengths, and they help with each other's weaknesses."

"You do know the breed well."

He chuckled. "My *ima* didn't approve of my focus being on the dogs. She thought I should use my talents to better the sheep breed." He rolled his eyes. "Truth be told, I enjoy the dogs much more."

"I wish I would have met Sarah." She smiled. "She sounds like an amazing woman."

"She was." He looked to the distant mountain. "And what of your parents?"

"My mother is not as wonderful as yours. She was very harsh on me. I assume it was because she wanted the best out of me." She pulled her arms around herself. "She was never abusive or hurtful, but we never seemed to be close. I was much closer with my father. Until…"

He lifted a brow at her. "Until?"

"Until he passed away." She let her gaze fall to the ground. "So, I know what it's like to lose a parent."

"I'm so sorry to hear that." He stepped closer to her. "I would have enjoyed meeting the man who raised such a fine woman."

She blushed.

They came near Jedidiah's camp and paused.

"May I ask what happened to him?"

Rebekah looked at Isaac. "He passed before I left. He had sustained an injury from a leopard attack a while back. Infections ebbed and flowed, but the last one carried him away from me."

"She's leaving out the best part." Hadiya seemed to appear out of nowhere. She was beaming at Rebekah.

Rebekah cut her glare at her handmaid.

"I was bringing Jedidiah a bowl of food Deborah prepared." The handmaid held the bowl up sheepishly.

Isaac glanced from Rebekah to her. "What do you mean?"

Hadiya ducked her head. "Forgive me, Mistress. I should not have spoken without permission."

"You have mine." Isaac set his shoulders. "What did she leave out?"

Hadiya raised her gaze to meet Rebekah's. "That

she was the one who saved her father from the mouth of the leopard."

His eyes widened on her. "You were?"

"I may have saved him from the mouth of the leopard." Rebekah sighed. "But I couldn't rescue him from the jaws of death."

Hadiya dipped her chin low and moved toward Jedidiah.

Isaac turned to face Rebekah. "You?"

She closed her eyes and shook her head. "It was a long time ago."

"But a leopard?"

"That wasn't the first beast I wrestled with, and it certainly wasn't the last." Emotions threatened to weigh her down. She picked up her steps toward the edge of the flock.

Isaac kept pace with her. "I'm sorry you had to handle everything you have, but my *abba* used to say it is our struggles that make us strong."

She turned toward him. "He told me the same when I met him."

They stood watching the light fade in the distance, and neither moved or spoke until several stars appeared above them.

Finally, Isaac turned to face her. "I suppose it's time to head in for the night."

Rebekah flushed under the cover of her veil. She knew exactly what he meant. Though the dowry had been paid and she had been delivered like cargo across the sands, their marriage could not be complete until it was consummated.

She ducked her head. "I suppose you're ready to look upon your purchase?"

He placed a single finger under her covered chin and lifted her face to meet his. "I wish to look upon my wife." He offered her his hand as he guided her to his tent.

Rebekah tucked her head to enter.

"This was my mother's." Isaac traced his fingers along the tent wall. "I took it when I departed from my *abba*. Many happy years were spent under this goatskin, and I pray it will have many more contained within it."

She smiled at the thought.

"It's just the two of us tonight." He motioned to her. "You can take that off if you'd like."

She reached up and carefully uncovered her face.

He stood still staring at her without saying a word for several heartbeats. He tried to hold his breath for fear he would wake up, and the beauty that stood before him would have been some wonderful dream.

With hesitation, he stepped forward and swept some of her dark hair off her shoulder. "You are so beautiful, Rebekah." Her name tasted sweet on his tongue. "Do you know the meaning of your name?"

She looked down. "In my land, it means a snare or noose."

He chuckled.

She glanced up at him, cheeks flaming.

"Not here. In our tongue, it means stall or hand-fed cattle."

She took a step back. "Are you calling me cattle?"

"No." He took a step toward her with both palms raised to her. "It's a very wonderful sign. The one cattle we raise in the stall and hand-feed is a choice animal. Your name here means life, not death."

She seemed frozen in the private workings of her mind.

Perhaps he had caused an unknown offense. He took another step closer. "I didn't mean to offend you."

She shook away distant thoughts.

He came so near they were less than a handbreadth apart. His eyes fell to her deep pink lips knowing exactly what he wanted. The temperature in the tent was rising even though it was dropping outside. "Rebekah?"

"Hmm?"

"May I kiss you?"

She parted her lips. "Yes," she whispered.

He closed the gap between them and let his lips dance softly on hers. He pulled back just far enough to look into her eyes.

She stared back with fire in hers.

He leaned in close and kissed her again with more desire and passion.

Rebekah melted into him.

Isaac wrapped his arms around her waist and pulled

her in even closer.

She yielded herself completely to him as he sealed their marriage with the cord of love's bonds.

Chapter 22

*"Therefore a man shall leave his father and his
mother and hold fast to his wife, and they shall
become one flesh."
-Genesis 2:24*

Beerlahairoi, 2025 B.C.
Rebekah

Early morning light peeked through the tent flap and
danced over Rebekah's face. Without opening her
eyes, she smiled to herself not fully understanding the
reason behind it.

There had been no week-long feast to celebrate
her marriage. No field full of family and friends to
rejoice with the new couple. No platters stacked high
with choice foods nor cups overflowing with wine and
other strong drink. She had been carried to Isaac and
embraced all alone in the arms of her husband.

She thought back to Eliezer's story of Adam and
Eve. They had no marriage feast either. No family to

attend it. The two of them were alone together celebrating their union. She smiled, hoping Eve felt as content as she did in that moment.

"Is my beautiful bride dreaming of some wonderful adventure?" Isaac's voice was smooth and close to her ear. She felt the heat of his body laying behind her. She kept her eyes closed, but couldn't fight the corners of her mouth rising higher. "Actually, I was thinking how we are like Adam and Eve."

"You know the story?"

She rolled over to look him in the eyes. "Eliezer told me many stories on our journey."

"Did he?"

She nodded.

"Did you enjoy them?"

"Most of them." She quieted and looked around the room. "You said this tent belonged to your mother. What was she like?"

He sat up on his elbow and traced lines on her bare arm. "She had such fire and was so beautiful. In fact, she was the most beautiful woman I had ever met in my entire life."

Rebekah winced.

"That was until I met you." He smiled playfully at her.

Heat rose into her cheeks and up through her temples.

He leaned down to kiss her softly, and then again with more desire. When he released his hold on her, he eased back and his hand traveled to her stomach. "I can't wait for the day you become a mother."

All at once, time seemed to halt for Rebekah. The tent spun around her as the full weight of Isaac's desire came crashing down on her. She had lost her father to infection, been scooped up, nearly taken in an ambush, forced to part with her most beloved companion, and transported across the world all without realizing from the moment she came home from the wilderness for the last time her female flow had ceased to return. She had not touched a leaf of shepherd's purse since then, but its effects had lingered for nearly a year. No flow meant no children.

She blinked herself back to the moment, finding Isaac staring back at her with concern etched deep in his face. There were no words to tell him that he had purchased a faulty bride. In a matter of one night, he had taken her heart and sealed it up in his calloused hands. How could she take away his one longing? How could Elohim give him a woman who would not fulfill the foretold blessing?

She attempted a smile, but it was halfhearted to say the least. "I suppose you must be hungry."

He furrowed his brow further, but then relaxed. "Starving."

She sat up and reached for her garments. Pulling them roughly over her head, she dressed and brushed through her hair with her fingers. "Forgive me." She hurried around the room. "I should have risen long ago to prepare something for you."

He stood and reached for her. His deep eyes searched hers. "Is everything well?"

"O-o-of course." She failed in hiding the tremor in her voice.

"Don't worry about the meal." He turned her into himself to hold her close.

Rebekah trembled all over.

"You're shaking." He lifted a hand to brush away the strains of hair sticking to her face. "And you're covered in sweat. Are you sure you are not ill?"

She shook her head. "I'm well." She smiled a fake smile again. "I'm just worried about taking care of you."

He hugged her for a long moment.

Rebekah wished a simple embrace could wash away her trouble.

"You will have plenty of time to learn," he whispered into her thick hair. "I don't expect you to be perfect."

If only you knew just how imperfect I was.

He held her out. "Take a few moments to properly prepare yourself. I'm going to see to Jedidiah and your women. Come out when you're ready."

Women. Hadiya and Deborah's faces flashed in her mind. "Could you send them into me?"

Isaac hesitated at the door, he held the flap open and stared at her for several heartbeats. "As you wish." He ducked out.

Rebekah twisted her hands and created a track in the large rug.

"Mistress?" Hadiya's call finally came at the door.

"Come in."

Hadiya and Deborah ducked into the tent and stood there.

Rebekah waved them in and offered them pillows to sit on.

They obeyed.

Rebekah remained standing and simply stared at them.

Hadiya was the first to break the silence. "Isaac said you sent for us?"

"I did." She bowed her head. "I fear I have a grave problem with which I was hoping you two could assist me."

Deborah rose to stand beside her. "We would do anything for you, child."

Rebekah wrapped her arms around herself. "I think there is a problem with my…" she hesitated and wrapped her midsection tighter, "…my umm well, my flow."

Deborah stole a glance at Hadiya. "What makes you think so?"

Rebekah stared at Hadiya.

The handmaid stood and folded her hands in front of herself. "I think you should tell her, Rebekah."

Deborah put her hands on her broad hips. "Tell me what?"

Rebekah looked at her nurse. "Each year I went to the wilderness, I took an herb with me. I was told by the priestesses at the temple it would hold back my flow. It was one less thing I had to contend with in the wilderness."

Deborah cut her glare at Hadiya. "You knew about this?"

She nodded. "Rebekah told me my first night under your roof."

Deborah shifted her focus to Rebekah. "I nursed you for years and guided you into womanhood. The thanks I get for it all is you hide this from me, yet reveal it to a servant?"

Rebekah folded into herself. "I wasn't trying to hide anything from you. I was hiding from *Ima*. If she found out what I was doing, she would have forbidden me from returning to the wilderness and forced me to become a wife."

"I hate to be the one to break the news to you, child, but you are no longer a shepherdess. You are a wife now."

Realization dawned on Rebekah like an unwanted new day. "I guess it's only fitting." She sighed and crumbled to the floor. She pulled her knees up to her chest and hugged them. "*Abba* forced Laban to be a shepherd and now I'm being forced to be a wife." She rocked back and forth. "I've gone from leading sheep in the fields to becoming someone's prized ewe. Only to grow large with child every year until I can no longer produce."

Hadiya sat beside her. "That's if we can get your flow started again."

She looked up at her handmaid. "I promise," she pleaded. "I haven't touched the stuff since I came back home. I don't know why my flow has dried up."

Deborah crossed her arms. "What did you take?"

"Shepherd's purse." She looked up. "Only during the months away from home and always in the quantity I was shown. I was always so careful."

Hadiya's attention perked up.

Rebekah watched her. "What is it?"

"I just remembered something that might help." She looked back at her. "Of course, I have no idea how to get our hands on it."

"What?"

"Pennyroyal. You steep the leaves just like shepherd's purse. I've heard it work for some whose flow had dried and… other uses."

"Do you really think it'll work?"

She shrugged. "I don't know, but it's worth a shot."

Deborah clicked her tongue. "That herb is even more dangerous than shepherd's purse. I don't think you should take anything. I think you should tell Isaac the truth."

Rebekah stood. "And risk having him send me away? Send us all away?" She shook her head. "No. We will find a way to get to a market."

"Rebekah?" Isaac's deep voice called from outside

the tent. "There is someone I'd like you to meet."

Rebekah looked to the two other women.

Both shrugged and held up their hands.

"I'll be right there," she called back.

"Here, let's fix you up." Hadiya stood and adjusted her dress and hair.

The three women exited the tent and sought out Isaac.

When they found him, he stood near the pen with a taller man.

"Ahh, there she is." Isaac waved Rebekah closer while the other two women remained where they were. "Rebekah, I'd like to introduce you to my brother, Ishmael."

The man bowed toward her. "It's a pleasure."

She bowed back. Ishmael reminded her a lot of Isaac and even more of their father. "The pleasure is all mine."

"Isaac, why didn't you tell me your father's servant was sent with the task to find such a beauty?" His gaze swept over her, but it was with approval.

Isaac beamed. "He obeyed Elohim. Beauty was merely in addition to her character."

"Well," Ishmael rubbed his hands together, "I'm here for my dog."

"Right." Isaac let him into the gate.

The pack of puppies bound toward them with yelps of joy.

Isaac tussled several of them and finally scooped

one of the bundles of energy into his arms. "I think Adena here will make a fine addition to your guard." He adjusted the solid form of the dog in his arms. "She shows much more of the nurture protective instinct which means she might stay tighter to your home instead of seeking out trouble." He held her out to his brother.

Ishmael lifted the dog to inspect her. "Can't say I know much about dogs, but if you say she's the one for me, then I'll take her."

Rebekah watched the exchange with curiosity. "How many flocks do you have?"

Ishmael looked at her with amusement. "I don't raise sheep."

"Oh, forgive me." Her cheeks flushed. "I only arrived just yesterday. I'm afraid I don't know very much of your family."

Ishmael cut a glance at Isaac. "It's alright, my dear. No, I actually live in Kadesh."

Images of a market sent hope rising up in her. "Kadesh? Does your city have a large bazaar?"

"One of the biggest around." He shifted the dog to under his massive arm. "You can find all that you could ever need there."

She looked over her shoulder at her nurse and handmaid.

Their eyes were wide.

She turned back. "I'd very much like to see your city."

Isaac furrowed his brow. "But you just arrived here."

Rebekah's heart raced when she saw the hurt in his eyes. "What I meant to say was that it would be nice to visit Ishmael in his home since he graced us with a visit here."

Isaac relaxed somewhat. "I see."

"What a splendid idea." Ishmael slapped his younger brother's back. "We'd love to have you and your new bride for a visit. Then you will finally get to meet my wife, and the two of them can get to know each other as well."

Isaac kept his gaze on Rebekah. "Thank you for the offer. It would bring us great pleasure."

"Good." He hoisted the dog higher in his arm. "Then I shall see you soon."

Rebekah watched Ishmael leave with the squirming bundle in his hands. She turned to see Isaac staring at her.

"I guess there are a few more stories I need to fill you in on."

She smiled. "I would like that very much."

Chapter 23

"The wisest of women builds her house,
but folly with her own hands tears it down."
-Proverbs 14:1

Kadesh, 2025 B.C.
Rebekah

Rebekah wasted no time in begging Isaac for a visit to see Ishmael in Kadesh. As soon as things were cleared with Jedidiah, the two, along with Hadiya, made the journey to the nearby city.

Isaac leaned over to Rebekah as they walked. "I don't understand why you insisted on bringing your handmaid for a simple visit."

"Ishmael mentioned the large market," she kept her voice low. "I want to do some trading, and there is no finer eye than Hadiya's when it comes to quality."

"I can supply whatever you need, if you simply let me know."

She swallowed a rising lump in her throat. "I'm sure you know your way around a market, but you wouldn't want to spend your time choosing women's garments, would you? I mean, I lost all my clothes in the raid. The only dress I brought with me belonged to Keturah."

He thought on her words. "I suppose you're right."

Hope rose a little higher. "I was thinking maybe Ishmael's wife could escort us through the market while you men reclined and talked. I'm sure you don't get much chance to have your brother all to yourself."

Isaac hesitated. "If I didn't know better, I would think you were planning to escape from me."

She put her hand on her chest. "Me? Surely you jest. I simply wanted to make the most of our trip to Kadesh. I thought the trip to the market would give me a chance to get to know Ishmael's wife." She continued her pace. "I think the sun has gotten to your mind." She attempted a faint smile.

Isaac returned his gaze to the horizon.

The rest of the trek was made in silence as Rebekah planned her next steps, including slipping Hadiya her last few coins.

When they arrived in Kadesh, Rebekah could hear the call of the market street, but knew she had to be cunning or her prize would not be won.

Isaac took them down the streets until they came to a large villa situated in a massive garden. The entire complex was surrounded by a tall iron fence.

Rebekah took in the immense sight. It was not the first time she had seen such a villa for there were many in the city of Haran, but this would be her first opportunity to be invited inside.

As they made it to the gate, a familiar sight greeted them. A large ball of energy came running toward them with her huge tail wagging.

"Adena." Isaac bent to get a better look at the animal through the iron rails. "Look how much you've grown in only a few short weeks."

The dog bounded playfully near her former master.

A guard came up behind her with a curious glare at the trio. "May I help you?"

Isaac stood tall. "My name is Isaac, and this is my wife Rebekah. We are here to visit my brother, Ishmael."

The guard looked down at the tumbling puppy and back at Isaac. "Master Ishmael did say to expect your company." He reached for the latch.

"I'll bring them in." Ishmael appeared behind the guard. He put a firm hand on the man's shoulder. "My brother instructed me to bring in any guests by the dog so she gets used to who is family and who is foe." He turned to give Isaac a wink.

"Glad to see you remembered."

Ishmael unlatched the gate and led the three of them inside, walking past the dog seeming to ignore her.

Isaac held his head high, but kept his eye on his former puppy. "How's she fairing?"

Ishmael maintained his forward gaze. "She is happy to be here, and the entire house fell in love with her at first sight. I did as you instructed and introduced her to my wife and mother first and then to the guards and servants." He stole a quick glance down at her running beside them. "She is kept here in the garden with the rotating guard as you suggested. I think she's made an excellent addition."

"Good work." Isaac resisted the urge to reward the puppy. "Keep it up and with time she will grow into a fine sentinel."

Ishmael guided them into the villa, leaving the dog playfully bounding at the door behind them.

Rebekah's eyes feasted on the luxury surrounding her. The evidence of Ishmael's wealthy state was palpable. Servants floated around them performing odd tasks. The floors, walls, and rooms were filled with fine pieces of art and comfort and all were meticulously tidy.

She raised the hem of her simple dress a little higher so as not to bring the filth of the outside in to stain the perfection among which she walked. Her chest felt a little tight thinking of how she would be received. She had scrubbed the only garment she owned until it was close to its original beauty, but it severely paled in comparison to her surroundings.

When they made it to a back room, two women

lounged on lush couches. Their beauty was so fair, Rebekah mistakenly thought she was looking upon another piece of art instead of real life. It wasn't until they moved to stand that she realized she must be in the presence of Ishmael's mother and wife. The two Egyptian beauties could have stepped out of a mural.

They came to stand on either side of Ishmael.

"*Ima*. Benemba. I'd like to present Isaac and his new bride, Rebekah."

Benemba dipped her head in respect.

The older woman, who Rebekah assumed was Hagar, merely nodded her recognition.

Rebekah bowed deeply allowing her gaze to drift to the mosaic flooring of several prancing antelope.

Isaac bowed. "We are humbled to be here."

Hagar looked around the couple to the woman standing silently behind them. "Who is this?" Her eyebrows lifted high. "Taken another wife already?"

Ishmael shot a glance at his mother; his face reddened. "*Ima*, don't speak in such a way to our guests. This is Rebekah's handmaid."

Hadiya bowed as deep as she could go without laying prostrate on the ground.

"As if we don't have enough servants to serve us?"

"Bringing her was my idea," Rebekah started, but stopped when she watched Isaac glare at her. She bit her lip. Of course, it wasn't her place to explain.

Isaac turned to Ishmael. "What my wife was trying to say was that she was hoping your wife would show them the market you spoke of. I'm afraid she lost her belongings along her journey and is eager to replace some of them." He flicked his head to Hadiya. "She claims her maid has a fine eye."

Hagar's right eyebrow rose higher. "Does she, now?"

Rebekah simply nodded. Maybe it wasn't too late to back out of her plan. She didn't count on so much attention being drawn to Hadiya or the simple request to visit the bazaar. She thought of the desire in Isaac's eyes when he spoke of children and how she had still not welcomed her feminine flow. She squared her shoulders, resolve set in her heart.

"Hadiya has the finest eye I've ever been witness to, and she can haggle with the best merchants in any town." She stole a quick glance at Isaac hoping he would not stay cross with her for long. Her gaze turned to Ishmael. "I was hoping your lovely wife could accompany us to the market while you enjoyed a private visit with your brother before the meal."

Ishmael looked to his wife, then to Isaac, and finally back to Rebekah. "Wonderful idea." He clapped his hands. "I am sorry to hear you lost your belongings during your travel." He rubbed his bearded chin. "Allow me to send along my personal guard and have the merchants put your purchases on my account."

Isaac stepped forward with outstretched hands. "We couldn't possibly accept such generosity. We merely came for a—"

Ishmael put up a hand to silence his brother. "Please. It would be my honor." He waved his hand and laid it on his chest. "Think of it as a wedding present from me. Since I did not get the pleasure of attending your feast."

"You're not the only one." Isaac rolled his eyes.

Ishmael's eyes grew wide. "You did not attend your own wedding feast?"

Isaac shook his head. "*Abba* held a short feast for Rebekah without my presence." He turned to his wife. "But feast or no feast. It doesn't change our status."

She beamed at the gentleness in his eyes.

Ishmael chuckled. "Oh, *Abba*. What a crazy fool you've become." He shook his head. "I shall send for your guard. You women can leave at once so you may be back before the evening meal." He moved to put a hand on Isaac's shoulder. "It seems my brother and I have much to speak of."

It was only moments later that Rebekah found herself being escorted by Hagar, Benemba, and two of Ishmael's guards through the streets of Kadesh.

The sounds and sights of the market drew near to them as they made their way toward it. Merchants' calls mingled in the air with the scents of spices and herbs. Varying types of animals and people made their way up and down the market street each protesting or bargaining.

Rebekah's eyes searched every booth they passed, hoping for some clue as to where she could find the prized herb she sought.

Hadiya's gaze was just as intense, though she was able to cover her intention under the guise of a judgmental eye.

Hagar and Benemba whispered among themselves as the group wandered. Though their voices were kept in hushed tones, Rebekah couldn't help but pick up pieces of their conversation. Especially when their remarks regarded her.

Hagar glanced over her shoulder to Rebekah. "Beauty won't purchase her affection for long if she can't keep her tongue from wagging."

Benemba hadn't agreed with her mother-in-law, but she hadn't come to Rebekah's defense either. She simply remained with her lips shut up like a sealed tomb.

When Hagar realized Rebekah had moved closer to hear them, she switched into a foreign tongue Rebekah assumed was the language of their birth.

Rebekah glanced at Hadiya whose gaze shifted to a nearby cloth seller whose booth was set up next to a spice merchant. Rebekah nodded and moved in that direction.

The Egyptian beauties were drawn along unaware with them.

Rebekah made sure to fain interest as she fingered the samplings. She held up a dress to Hadiya who took her time inspecting the garment. By drawing out the process, Rebekah hoped the other two women would grow impatient.

The longer she drew out her inspection, the more she could see Hagar's patience thin. The older woman's sandaled foot tapped as she crossed her arms. Her glances wavered to other booths. She huffed several times.

Finally, the waiting became too great for Hagar. "Well, are you going to make a decision or move on?"

Rebekah showed the women the dress. "We are just not sure." Her eyes flicked to Hadiya as she backed up. "I do not wish to take advantage of Ishmael's generous offer so we are making sure each purchase is worthy." She held up the garment. "What do you think of this one?"

While the two women's attention moved to the material, Rebekah watched Hadiya subtly speak with the nearby spice merchant who shook his head and returned to his group of patrons. Hadiya took a step nearer to Rebekah and gave a sorrowful shake of her head.

Rebekah felt her heart drop a little.

Hadiya's silent glance flew to another stall down the way. Its tables overflowed with piles of spices and herbs.

Rebekah nodded before turning her attention back to the other women.

Hagar rubbed the material between her delicate fingers. "It doesn't seem to be a very sturdy structure." Her eyes flicked to Hadiya. "It seems your maid hasn't a good eye for quality after all." She deposited the garment on the table. "We shall continue on." She moved across the way.

Hadiya kept behind the others.

Rebekah stopped with Hagar at the booth she had spotted.

"There, you see," she pointed to the material, "much better."

Rebekah took a piece in her hands and rubbed her callused fingertips over the linen. "You have excellent taste."

Hadiya moved behind them to the spice booth.

Rebekah attempted to keep her focus on the garment in her hands, but it meant losing Hadiya in the crowded street. "This is a fine dress indeed." She held up the garment to her body hoping her adjusted position would give her a chance to spot Hadiya. It didn't. She had momentarily lost her in the sea of booths and people.

Hagar touched the dress and hummed to herself. "We can find even better further down."

Rebekah glanced toward the spice booth and watched Hadiya reappear near them. She observed the woman nod her head and keep it down for a moment before raising it and pointing to her hip.

Rebekah's heart fluttered. She turned her attention back to Hagar who held a look of disapproval. "I think this will do fine." She blushed. "I will not be hosting such fine guests as you do. I fear I need garments and materials that would be better suited for the harshness of the fields."

"I suppose you're right." Hagar looked to Benemba and then back to Rebekah. "We can't all be as fortunate to marry successful men, now can we?" She batted her long lashes.

Rebekah swallowed her next words, resigning to the woman's attempts at judgment, and smiled. "These will serve me well."

"At least they will be better than your useless handmaid." Her glare cut at Hadiya who stood about a stone's throw from them merely watching them speak.

Rebekah fought every fiber of her being's urge to defend her most trusted companion. If her plan was going to come to completion, she needed them to finish in the market and return to the villa without raising suspicion of their ulterior motive. "I do apologize for my insistence on her accompanying me."

Hagar sighed. "Well, at least she hasn't caused any harm. I've dismissed slaves for much less." She shifted her body toward the merchant and gave Ishmael's information to add the purchases to his account.

Rebekah shot a painful and apologetic look to her handmaid.

Hadiya's shoulders came up slightly as she closed her eyes.

The women finished their purchases and retreated to the complex to join the men for a feast fit for royalty.

Epilogue

"And Isaac prayed to the LORD for his wife, because she was barren. And the LORD granted his prayer, and Rebekah his wife conceived."
-Genesis 25:21

Beerlahairoi, 2005 B.C.
Rebekah

Rebekah sat on the banks of the shallow stream watching Hadiya wash her linen wrap.

The maid rang out the material in her hand. "You have that look again."

"Sorry." She shook her head. "Hope seems to be one thing I can't kill."

"Hope is not a weakness, Mistress." She dipped the garment into the water again. "And it shouldn't be something you attempt to kill." She wrung the cloth a final time. "You were thinking of children again?"

She nodded.

Hadiya flapped the garment out and laid it to dry on the large boulder next to her. "Maybe there is something else we can try?"

Rebekah sighed. "In the last twenty years, we've been to every spice merchant, physician, and temple in the surrounding cities." She dipped her hand into the flowing water. "I don't think there is anything left for us to try." She lifted her fingers and shook them. "The sands of time are shifting away from me as well. Soon it will be too late to try anymore."

Hadiya put her hand on her broad hip. "What about Sarah?"

Rebekah's attention came up. "What about her?"

"Didn't you say she bore Isaac when she was in her one hundredth year?"

"Well yes, but…I mean she did, but…well that was a special circumstance."

"What makes her circumstance any more special than yours?"

Rebekah thought about the question. She couldn't come to an answer.

Hadiya returned to her washing.

Rebekah sat quietly listening to the sounds of the brook. "I suppose I should head in. It's almost time for the sacrifice."

The younger woman nodded. "I'll finish up here."

Rebekah stood and brushed the dust from her dress. She walked toward the collection of tents she called home for the last twenty years. Under Isaac's hand, their flocks had prospered, and he had amassed many shepherds under his management. They added more servants to help with the daily provisions, and many had expanded their tents under their master's gentle and humble hand.

The couple had gained the respect of those around them and those who resided in the wilderness with them. The only thing missing from their lives was the one promise that still remained unfulfilled. They had not expanded their own tent to include children.

Rebekah's heart was heavy as she took in the familiar sight. Young ones of free and bond played together among the shadows of the growing tent city. Hand helped hand and smile was exchanged with smile among the people under their watch. She had all she could dream of, but her arms and her womb remained empty.

About an arrow's shot away from the tent, Isaac stood clearing off their family altar. The simple structure had been set up shortly after her arrival. It reminded her of the one she had first seen in Shechem built by her father-in-law, Abraham. Isaac had taken unhewn stones and constructed his own altar to offer sacrifices to Elohim.

Though he never required anyone to join him in the daily sacrifices, Isaac welcomed any who chose to cease their work and spend time worshipping at the altar of Elohim. Rebekah had stood by his side every day for twenty years listening to his heartfelt prayers to the God of his father.

As she stood there this day, watching the choice animal burn, Isaac's words sunk deep into her soul.

"I pray most of all for my wife," her husband's words flowed as easily and freely as the stream she had spent the afternoon beside. "Elohim, I pray that You would fulfill Your promise and provide us a child to bless Your name."

Rebekah couldn't take it anymore. She closed her ears and her heart to his desperate pleas.

When the sacrifice was complete, the group moved back to the tents to prepare for the evening meal.

Rebekah sat in her tent with Isaac watching him consume the offerings of Deborah and Hadiya. She had no desire to eat as she stared at the bowls and platters before them.

"Wife?"

Her gaze came up to see Isaac staring at her.

"Do you feel ill?"

She shook her head. "I'm well."

"Then why do you look as though this offering were a pit of serpents?"

"I was just thinking about something."

He adjusted to move closer to her. "Care to share your burden?"

She kept her gaze to the floor. "I was just wondering why you never took a concubine."

He set his bowl down and turned his body toward her. "When I saw you, my love, all other women lost their allure to me."

She closed her eyes, fighting the burn of tears. "I wish you had."

Isaac reached over to tip her chin up and waited for her to open her eyes. "Why do you say such a thing?"

"Because if you had, then maybe you would be an *abba* by now." Tears fell down in large drops.

He wiped them with his thumb. "My sweet wife, you know that plan never ends well."

Her thoughts went immediately to his father's other son, Ishmael, and the concubine-mother who had been cast out. Isaac would never do such a thing.

"I could never lie with another." He set his honey eyes on her. "Never."

Bile rose up in her like venom. "But if you don't, we shall never fulfill the promise. With each passing day, it grows more impossible."

"The word impossible is not found in the language of Elohim's ability." His fingers moved up and down her cheek. "He will see fit to fulfill His promise in His time."

Rebekah brushed away his hand and rose. She walked out of the tent into the cool night air. The sun had set and the stars and moon were so bright she could see far into the distance. Her feet took her through the paths between the tents and out into the open.

Before she realized what she was doing, she found herself standing before the simple family altar. No idols sat there expecting a food offering. There were no bowls for incense. Only a stack of natural stones layered on each other stood before her.

She thought about the day's sacrifice burning on top. The stones were stained with the blood of every previous offering that had laid there before. The stains of twenty years' worth of Isaac's unanswered prayers stared back, mocking her.

She lifted her fists and struck the pile of rocks. "You are supposed to be the One Who Sees!" She pounded her fists against the jagged stones. "Why don't You listen to him?" Her gaze shot up to the sky. Tears stung at her eyes begging to be released. "You saw Hagar in this place, but You turn deaf ears to the son of the only man with whom You speak. You turn blind eyes to the wife whom You dragged across the sands to be his." She melted to the ground and pressed her forehead to the cool stones. "Why don't You see me?"

She wrapped her arms around herself giving into the sobs that tore at her throat. "Why don't You see me?" Wailings and sobs racked her body as she rocked against the altar. "Please. See me."

The next day, Rebekah completed her chores in silence. Something between relief and grief settled inside her. She had spoken her peace to the God of her husband, but there had been no response. No voice from above, no strange visitor, not even a dream to deliver her an answer. The invisible god of Abraham had remained silent.

When the sun reached its height of the day, Rebekah retreated to her quiet tent to rest. She lay on a pile of soft skins. Her body ached worse than she could remember. She felt as tired as if she had traveled all day and night without reprieve. Not having an explanation, she marked it to her mental battle with the unseen.

She noticed the edge of her garment and sandals covered in a thick layer of mud. An unseasonal rain the night before had mixed with the soil and left Rebekah covered while she worked with the young lambs in the pen. Dark spots were splattered down her legs. She moved to wipe at them. Some came off easy, but some wouldn't budge. Those spots were not the dark color of mud, but held a crimson hue.

Odd. It almost looks like… blood.

During her work, she hadn't encountered any injured animal. She sat up to examine the rest of her body seeking out an injury. It only took a few moments before she discovered the source. She was not injured, but had succumbed to the flow which visited every other woman with each cycle of the moon. Though she had not greeted this stream in over twenty years.

The tent flap peeled back revealing Hadiya.

"Mistress?"

Rebekah looked up at her with a smile spread wide across her lips. "I'm bleeding."

Hadiya rushed to her side. "Do you need assistance?" She sought out a wrap. "Should I get Isaac?"

Rebekah reached out to grab her arm. "I'm not injured."

Hadiya looked at Rebekah until realization dawned. "Your flow?"

She nodded. "It has returned."

"What did you take?"

"Nothing." She shook her head. "It just started today."

Hadiya held her head. "I don't understand. We tried every possible herb and treatment man can offer, yet one day it just starts up again?"

Rebekah released her grip and held onto her aching midsection. "I don't think this was man's doing."

Hadiya arched an eyebrow.

"I think it was Elohim."

"What makes you say that?"

"I prayed to Him last night, at Isaac's altar."

"I thought only Isaac and Abraham could talk to Elohim."

"I thought so too." She hugged the sharpening pains she couldn't deny.

"Well, let's get you wrapped up and mix you

something to help with the pain." She searched for a clean linen and handed it to her mistress.

Rebekah smiled despite the pain. Perhaps Elohim was finally working out His promise.

Months came and went for Rebekah as she welcomed her feminine flow. Each time reminded her that her body was ready to be the fertile soil in which Elohim could plant His promised seed.

After three cycles, she sought out Hadiya. "Am I doing something wrong?"

The woman shrugged. "Just because your body is ready doesn't mean Elohim is."

"I thought it would be so easy. Somehow get my flow unblocked and then welcome a child."

"It's not always like that. Sometimes it takes a while."

After a full harvest season had come and gone, Rebekah's faith began to waver.

One day, she sat next to Hadiya watching her prepare dough for the next round of bread.

"Are you sure?" The maid kneaded the dough.

"Positive." Rebekah sighed. "My flow has dried up again." She drew up her knees to her chest and put her chin upon them. "Nothing in two moon cycles."

"Maybe it will return again."

"I don't have another twenty years to wait."

"Perhaps it's time to speak with Isaac."

"Speak to me about what?" Isaac appeared near the fire.

Rebekah looked to her husband and then back to Hadiya.

"Rebekah," his eyes remained fixed on her, "is there something you wish to discuss with me?"

"I…uh…" she faltered, staring at her handmaid.

Isaac's attention flicked to the other woman and then back to his wife. "Hadiya, would you excuse us please."

"As you wish, Master." She covered the dough and walked away from the fire.

Isaac moved to sit down next to Rebekah. "Now, what do you have on your heart?"

She looked up into his gentle glance. Her words remained locked behind the rising lump in her throat. How could she put a seal on the tomb of their infertility? She glanced at the fire.

"Rebekah?"

She looked back at him. The light from the fire reflected back in the oasis of his honey eyes. She was going to break his heart. Maybe he would send her away like his father had sent Hagar into the wilderness.

"Love, I can see the pain etched clear on your face." He moved closer. "Please speak to me."

"I'm never going to give you children."

His head hung low for several moments before he set his gaze on her. "That's not your concern."

"What are you talking about?" She waved her arms. "It's obvious I'm as barren as an old ewe. Your father purchased a defective bride. Your God chose a scarred wife."

Isaac shook his head and moved closer to her. He wrapped his massive arm around her and drew her as close to his side as he could. "Man, nor woman, can seal an open womb and neither can they open a sealed one. It is only Elohim, and Him alone who decides when life springs from the womb."

She looked down and shook her head. "You know I cried out to Him." She huffed. "I actually thought He had finally answered because my flow returned for a few months. But I guess He decided to withdraw His hand because it hasn't returned this moon's cycle or last."

"Two cycles?"

She nodded.

"But it returned before that?"

"For a few cycles." She looked up into his intense gaze. "A full harvest's worth."

"And you haven't eaten many meals recently."

She looked up at him with furrowed brows.

"I may not see all like Elohim, but I notice when my wife has lost her hunger."

She thought back to the platters of food she'd been

offered in the past few months. Though the food had not changed, her desire for them had. She thought it was simply her struggles that kept her stomach churning.

"I don't see what that has to do with anything."

His smile broadened. "My sweet wife, don't you see?"

She shook her head.

"Hope has taken root in you. Elohim has finally answered our prayers." He looked to her stomach.

She looked down at her midsection and then back to him. "You really think so?"

He nodded.

"Isaac, Rebekah," Jedidiah's call sounded in the distance. "Come quick."

The two got up and rushed outside to find Jedidiah waving to them from the pens.

Jedidiah knelt beside one of their dogs, Hava.

Rebekah opened the gate and let herself in. "Is she injured?"

"No, I think it's time."

Isaac shut the gate behind himself. "Puppies?"

Jedidiah nodded.

"Well, let us get ready to welcome new life into our family." Isaac winked at Rebekah.

Her hands moved to her stomach as she stood watching the whelping mother. This would not be the only new life they would welcome. She felt a well of new hope spring up inside as she thought about the new life growing in her womb. Elohim had heard her prayers, and those of her husband. The One Who Sees had finally seen her.

Want to find out what happens next?

Rebekah's boys were an answer to prayer.
Now they've become a nightmare.

For twenty years, Rebekah prayed for her womb to be open. When the answer finally came in the form of twin boys, Rebekah's hope was restored in the God she was learning to trust. But with their constant fighting and stark personalities, will her tent hold up under the tension of the two boys? Or will their differences drive them apart?

Jacob wanted a simple life of shepherding like his father before him. But when his mother comes up with a plan to put him ahead of his brother, he can't resist the temptation. The result is a threat on his life. Now, he must flee from his twin brother before it's too late. Will his uncle provide protection in the place of his mother's birth or lead him on a path of destruction?

Follow along as both learn that hope can be a dangerous thing in *The Hope*.

Also by Jenifer Jennings:

Special Collections and Boxed Sets

Biblical Historical stories from the Old Testament to the New, these special boxed editions offer a great way to catch up or to fall in love with Jenifer Jennings' books for the first time.

Faith Finder Series: Books 1-3
Faith Finders Series: Books 4-6
The Rebekah Series: Books 1-3
Servant Siblings Series: Books 1-3

* * *

Faith Finders Series:

Go deeper into the stories of these familiar faith heroines.

Midwives of Moses
Wilderness Wanderer
Crimson Cord
A Stolen Wife
At His Feet
Lasting Legacy

* * *

The Rebekah Series:
Follow Rebekah on her faith journey through life.

The Stranger
The Journey
The Hope

* * *

Servant Siblings Series:
They were Jesus' siblings,
but they become His followers.

James
Joseph
Assia
Jude
Lydia
Simon
Salome

* * *

Paul's Patrons Series:
Little known supporters of Paul's ministry have their
own stories to tell.

Raging Sea
Warring Church

Find these titles at your favorite retailer or at:
jeniferjennings.com/books

Thank you!

Hubby, thank you for your gentleness and support through every step of my writing journey. In the hard times, you are there to keep me on my feet. In the good times, you are there to rejoice with me. I'm so glad we get to do this life together.

Kids, even as young as you are, you still find your own ways to encourage and inspire me in my writing. I hope one day you will look back on the days I spend at my computer as opportunities for me to make our time together special. I love you both so much.

Clay County Word Weavers, thank you for your excitement over each project I bring to the table. Your words of encouragement and helpful critique drive me to keep writing. It is an honor to serve as our chapter's President.

Jill, my fabulous editor and huntress of typos and errors. Thank you for putting in the hard work to refine each story. Without you, my readers would get stuck in the quicksand of mistakes instead of enjoying the story.

Jenifer's Jewels, my wonderful ARC team, you guys and gals are amazing. I love hearing from each of you before these stories are released to the public. Your excitement and eagerness keep me at my writing desk.

A special thank you to Gloria, Isabella, A.B., Jenna, Deborah, and Jill for your name suggestions. You have eternal bragging rights for helping name these wonderful people and creatures in my stories. I hope you smile when you see the names you suggested and hold a special place in your heart for these characters you had a hand in bringing to life.

Readers, I have the biggest appreciation for you. Without your devotion and hunger, I would have no reason to share my writing. I know it is God who has called me to write, but it is your patient eagerness that keeps me sending stories out into the world. I pray that each one you read draws you a step closer to our awesome God.

About the Author

Jenifer Jennings writes Historical novels that immerse readers in ancient worlds filled with Biblical characters and faith-building stories. Coming to faith in Jesus at seventeen, she spends her days falling in love with her Savior through the study of His Word. Jenifer has a Bachelor's in Women's Ministry and graduated with distinction while earning her Master's in Biblical Languages. When she's not working on her latest book, Jenifer can be found on a date with her hardworking husband or mothering their two children.

If you'd like to keep up with new releases, receive spiritual encouragement, and get your hands on a FREE book, then join Jenifer's Newsletter: jeniferjennings.com/gift

Printed in Great Britain
by Amazon

55764119R00126